DON'T THINK A SINGLE THOUGHT

DON'T THINK A SINGLE THOUGHT

Diana Cambridge

2019
Louise Walters Books

Don't Think a Single Thought
by Diana Cambridge

A catalogue card for this book is available from the British Library.

Produced and published in 2019
by Louise Walters Books

ISBN 978 1 999 7809 99
eISBN 978 1999 6305 08

Typeset in PT Serif 11pt by Blot Publishing
www.blot.co.uk

Printed and bound by Clays Ltd, Elcograf S.p.A.

Louise Walters Books
PO Box 755
Banbury
OX16 6PJ

For David

The Hamptons, 1963

She wakes. There's a second or two of comfort – the warm bed, the shimmering morning light, the sound of seagulls. There's even a pleasant residual muzziness from the sleeping pills the night before – then anxiety claws at her. Her stomach wrenches, her mind spins with fear.

Their Hamptons apartment is empty – her husband left for the city hours ago. She could make fresh coffee in the immaculate beach house kitchen, but that means getting out of bed.

'Try to put one leg out, then the other,' her therapist had urged last week, smiling, making a sort-of joke. She'd smiled back at him. But it can't be done. Her legs won't move. She clings to the quilt, buries her head in the pillow. Soon she'll reach for another pill.

'It's a vacation – the fresh air will do you good. Get you back in shape – you know. And we can hire a housekeeper – you won't have to do a thing except lie on the beach and read. That suit you?' That was a kind of joke, too, though in her nerved-up state she'd detected some criticism in her husband's words. He'd still commute to Manhattan, but reduce his time at the hospital.

Her therapist advised: 'Just lie on the beach, Emma, and don't think a single thought.'

She'd been ill for months with a mystery virus, flu-like symptoms that wouldn't go away, her energy falling all the time. Her weight had plummeted, and she'd had to abandon her job in favor of spending time in bed. They'd prescribed anti-depressants which didn't work. Tranquilizers were better... an expensive doctor would always let you have some, reluctantly of course. She wasn't an addict: it was occasional use only.

When she woke for the second time a few hours later, the sun was beating down; there was also a breeze. Could she manage the beach? Theirs was almost private, a stretch of powdery sand in front of their villa. She could hear the maid clattering about in the kitchen... she had to get away from the harsh domestic reproach. Showered, made-up, dressed in a pale yellow sun dress, she ventured into the kitchen.

'You startled me, Mrs. Bowden!' said the maid, a middle-aged woman in a flowery overall. 'What would you and Dr. Bowden like for tonight? I thought maybe baked salmon or herbed chicken with potatoes and vegetables, French style. Everything's fresh.'

'The chicken sounds wonderful, Maria,' Emma said, trying to inject enthusiasm into her voice. 'He'll be back about eight. He likes your lemon tart as well.'

'Oh, everybody likes that! Especially with thick cream. I've had some clients eat three helpings, one after the other.'

Have you?

Packing a bag with sunscreen, headache pills, a novel, she stepped out into the day.

Yes, it was gorgeous. Fine sand... waves drifting in, huge tubs of pink and white flowers along the edge of the beach. Far-apart loungers with little tables. A beach bar with uniformed butlers.

She lay on a lounger, closed her eyes. A butler came to ask her if she'd like anything, maybe iced coffee? When it arrived, she swallowed a couple of headache pills – she felt the familiar tight band forming round her eyes. The heat. She searched for half an Equanil in her bag, and gulped that too. The tablets... they didn't seem to work as well as they used to. She found another sliver of Equanil and added it to the pill she'd taken – and actually did begin to feel better, a little. The familiar, pleasant wooziness, the blurring of panic.

Children were playing a little distance from her, building sand up around one of them so before long you would be able to see only his head. She'd read... somewhere... this was dangerous. Children had died, been buried alive. Their hearts had stopped, crushed by the sand, while their faces still seemed to smile. Where was the mother of these children?

'Don't do that!' she called to them. They looked over, startled. 'It's dangerous. Stop... now. Where are your parents?'

'Over in the clubhouse.'

They made faces at each other, indicating she was crazy. She stood up.

'What are your parents' names? I'm going to speak to them.'

Now they looked nervous. 'Spencer. What for? We haven't done anything wrong.'

Feeling oddly strong, she marched into the clubhouse and found the Spencers.

Polite, with pleasant voices, they listened and nodded.

'Yes, of course – it's a silly thing for them to do. I'll come over with you now,' said Fiona Spencer, while George gulped back his highball.

They walked over to where she'd seen the children.

Nothing there. No one. Just the smooth beach. Had she...? Was she...?

'There they are!' said Fiona as her three children came running up. 'We don't want you burying each other in the sand – is that clear? This lady was perfectly right to come and see us.'

'But we didn't! She's made it up! She started shouting at us for nothing! We've been swimming and making sandcastles all the time. And we saw her talking to herself. She made it all up – didn't you? Didn't you?'

Three scornful kids' faces and a pitying adult one turned towards her.

'I think you kids should come up with me now,' said Fiona. 'It's about time for lunch. I'm sorry they were a nuisance.' They walked away.

Emma burst into quiet tears. She'd seen... she knew. She'd go back to the villa. Maria would have made the bed up. She'd pull the blinds down. Sleep... the bliss of sleep... until Jonathan came home. Then, bathed, groomed, she'd tell him... she'd tell him she was feeling better.

1937

The therapists in the children's unit where they'd sent Emma were always smiling, kind, detached. She was ten. She stayed there six months. It was to help her get over the accident, which she knows she'll never get over.

That school trip, walking in pairs, hand-in-hand on a coastal path – but not with her best friend. The best friend doesn't turn up. Instead, she's paired with a hated classmate – the only other girl on her own. A girl no one cares for. This girl, Moira, tells her a boy Emma likes is pretending to like her back, and has made fun of her.

'He thinks you look like a horse!' laughs this girl. 'It's even funnier you think he's keen on you.'

Emma snatches her hand away: the girl skids, screams and slides to her death over the cliff edge, into the ocean.

The school was charged with faulty care of the pupils – there should have been a teacher near every pair. Of course, this wasn't possible – and they'd warned the girls over and over again not to go near the cliff edge. The coastal authority was fined for not putting DANGER notices up and not repairing and fencing it off.

Emma, mired in horror, unable to get out of bed, needed hospital care. In a children's unit.

Every afternoon there was an hour of therapy, art and exercise. She was encouraged to write. She could write her feelings out. They didn't judge; they encouraged her, said she showed promise as a writer.

Her parents visited every other weekend. They were obsequious to the staff, and always seemed to be apologizing for Emma, as if she wasn't there.

Therapists tried to persuade her that what had happened was not her fault, never her fault. An accident: tragic, but an accident. Her life would heal itself, if she let it. She was a bright, pretty girl with a warm future ahead… the past would gradually recede. It would become the past.

No one from her school visited, not even the best friend who hadn't turned up on the day of the accident. She made friends among the other children at the hospital – not really friends. Everyone there seemed to hate their parents. That their own parents could have them "locked up in a loony bin" – their own parents! – created a permanent anger. Parents were the enemy. Everyone longed for the time of freedom. Not freedom to go home – freedom to move away, into a room of their own. Absolute freedom.

She began to "get better". It wasn't so much the influence of the hospital, but because she wasn't with her parents. She counted the years until she'd be free to leave home – five or six. That wasn't so long, if you counted up a whole life! She could hang on. Would hang on. Would bide her time.

Classes were small and the teachers kind – she kept

on with her writing and her artwork. At home, the accident was no longer mentioned. She knew that every year the dead girl's parents held a "vigil" for her somewhere by the ocean – how did that benefit anyone? But she applied herself to her studies and got herself to Vassar, and a room of her own.

She never went home again.

She sent cards.

THE HAMPTONS, 1963

'Your work and the people you love... those are the important things in life. The only important things.'

Who'd said that? A boyfriend, a long time ago. It seemed significant at the time, but now was ambiguous, almost without meaning.

She'd gone from being a successful writer of magazine short stories to... to writing advertising copy. And then not even that. Her writing work seemed to dry up. She'd been unwell. This holiday was supposed to revive her. They weren't short of money. But she liked earning her own, enjoyed the status of her career as a magazine journalist, now lost; had even enjoyed the terrified feeling she'd had just before giving a bookshop talk... it was ages since she'd done that.

'Emma. Em! Wake up, old girl! Daydreaming again? Have we any oat cakes for the cheese?'

'I did ask Maria to bring some – she must have forgotten,' she lied, holding up her glass for more champagne. Jonathan said it was good for her, and it was, until she woke at 3 a.m., heart racing.

'You must be feeling better if you're having a drink... fine, but remind her tomorrow, will you? I can't eat Brie without oat cakes.'

He took his briefcase into the room they called his "den" while she sat on the front stoop, enjoying the breeze. She heard what sounded like a bike being wheeled to the back, then the letterbox.

Wicked, selfish people who make things up get what they deserve.
This means YOU!!

At first glance it was comic, written on lined paper in a childish hand. She guessed straight away who it was from. Those kids she'd told off at the beach. Told off because they were burying each other in the sand – dangerously. How dare they send her this vicious letter?

She couldn't tell Jonathan – but the next day she'd damn well go see their parents again. She – a journalist, a writer – being treated like this! By some stupid, over-privileged kids! Fury made her hands shake. She took another sip of champagne. She took a sleeping pill.

'I'm going to bed, Jonathan. I'm tired. I guess I had too much sun.'

'Sleep well, Emma – the booze should help. I'm leaving early tomorrow, so won't wake you. Don't forget the oatcakes.'

The next morning she woke, stomach churning. She was going to challenge that couple with the vile letter from their kids. Calling her "wicked" and "selfish" because she'd stopped them from playing a dangerous game! She chose a pale pink cotton sundress, a necklace of darker pink wooden beads, Dior makeup and Chanel scent.

Made-up and ready, she began to feel nervous.

'My, you look nice, Mrs. Bowden,' said Maria. 'Going out for lunch? Tonight, I thought a rib of beef with a green salad and pan-fried potatoes, and a crème caramel with vanilla and butterscotch sauce. Would Dr. Bowden like that?'

'I'm sure he would,' she said. 'But could you remember to get some oatcakes for the cheese? They have them at the deli.'

'I'll try,' said Maria. 'If not, would crackers do?'

No, they wouldn't, she was tempted to say, but instead, 'Yes, I suppose so... or perhaps cheese straws? If you could make them, that would be even better.'

A theatrical sigh, then, 'Of course, Mrs. Bowden. See you later.'

Walking into the clubhouse, she spotted them immediately.

'Fiona!' she said, at her most vivacious. 'I hope you don't mind me coming over – I had a rather disturbing letter. Put through our door last night.'

She showed them. There was no answering sympathy.

'This isn't anything like the handwriting of any of our kids,' said Fiona. 'I'm sure they wouldn't do that, anyway. They're good kids. Was anyone else around when... yesterday, I mean? When you were on the beach?'

'No!'

The Spencers looked alarmed.

'Can I buy you a coffee or a drink, Mrs...?' offered George. 'I imagine this was a shock – but it's just a... I don't know.'

'Emma. Emma Bowden. Thank you. Perhaps a... Bloody Mary.'

Looking even more alarmed at this choice, they ordered the drink for her. She sipped. It was over-spiced.

'Thanks. I guess – they could have dictated it to someone else who wrote it?'

'No, really. I think what has happened is some other kid overheard and sent this as a prank. I'd try to forget it if I were you.' George again, soothing, jollying her along.

'You're not me. And I'll get to the bottom of it.'

They murmured a few platitudes, she downed the drink and said goodbye.

Walking back to her villa, she saw their children playing on the sand.

'I know it was you!' she shouted. 'Don't think you'll get away with it, either. Brats.'

She heard one starting to cry. She walked further down the beach and chose a light lunch in a beach bar. Shrimp cocktail, a small portion of pasta with fresh Italian sauce, a pistachio ice cream. A glass of chilled white wine.

The headache started up, but it was manageable with a painkiller. She was even enjoying staring out to sea, not thinking, not having to talk. Treating herself. Taking herself out to lunch. Not thinking.

1934

It's not as though they were even her real parents – she was adopted at eight. Her real mother had died, while Emma was fostered, from drink and drugs and depression. She'd tried to look after her children; it was too much for her. Their apartment was rough, in a slum area. Often her mother had been out all night, leaving Emma and two babies, Cathy and Mikey, alone, hungry, crying. She'll never forget the night welfare workers entered the cold rooms and carried her, her brother and sister away, into care.

They were gentle, but she screamed for her mother – she'd rather be with Mommy, despite everything, than strangers – where were they taking her? To elderly foster parents, frugal with food. Then she was adopted. Being shown around, displayed, given a lot of new clothes and toys when she preferred her old ones. A feeling of having to perform, smile, pretend.

She remembered being introduced to someone called Grandma, who had a kind, lined, smiling face... Emma astonished the adults with her clear greeting.

'Hello, Grandma! How are you today?'

'Sweet little thing – I never expected her voice to be so strong...'

'They couldn't have given you a lovelier girl, could

they?' her adoptive mother's sister said, with jealousy. There was a group of relatives standing around her, staring.

'But what happened to your proper mommy?' asked a small boy. Her face fell.

'I told you not to say anything!' she heard.

But there was always a feeling – she felt it, knew it – that she might do something bad. She knew – she thought – her parents were ashamed of her.

But she never saw them now. Never. That was the good thing about growing up. Once you had grown up.

THE HAMPTONS, 1963

'Emma? Sorry to disturb you... can I join you for a minute?' It was George Spencer. Reluctantly, she nodded. She was trying to forget she had shouted at his kids on the beach – they'd been frightening her, hadn't they? Doing something dangerous with the sand...

She was enjoying lunch by herself. She was on her second glass of wine. She felt better – better than she had in days, until he turned up.

'Ah... this is a bit difficult, but the kids were upset after you shouted at them this morning. Could I ask you not to approach them again? It is their vacation – and of course it's yours too – I feel a mistake has been made and I know it's worrying. What does your husband think?'

'He thinks the letter came from your kids.'

'Emma Bowden. Your name sounds familiar. Haven't you written short stories?'

'Yes.' She was thrilled.

'I have dabbled a bit myself. Not got anything published, though.'

She felt renewed, adventurous.

'I'm having a coffee. Would you like one?'

'Thanks, but no... I'm taking the family to lunch someplace up the coast. Look, can we... make a truce on the letter? I'm sure nothing else will happen.'

She said nothing, dejected by his turning down the coffee. She was considered an attractive woman. She was thirty-six. Thirty-six-itis – she'd heard of it. Marilyn Monroe was said to have died from it. Partly. 'Goodbye, Emma. We'll see you around.'

Walking back, she anticipated her cool bed, half a pill, the hours of being out of it until Jonathan returned from work.

When she got back, the villa was quiet. Maria had made cheese straws. There was a wonderful smell of baking. The table was laid for two, with blue napkins and candles, a glass tumbler of rose geraniums. Maria wouldn't be there to cook and serve dinner for hours. She was free to sleep.

Emma? Emma, is that you?

She woke, groggy... the voice, high, thin, bubbling with laughter, seemed to come from far away. It wasn't Jonathan. It was a child's voice. Terrified, she lay still.

Emma... I'm coming to see you... Emma... Hello? Hello?

The voice faded, as though it was on a phone line... she sat up, shaking. Had she imagined it?

It was so clear, so real... what time was it? Six o'clock – she'd been asleep for three hours. Maria would be here at seven to do dinner, then Jonathan back from work... she'd get up now. She tried to shake off that clear, laughing, sinister voice.

Showering, she left the bathroom door open, but the fear was receding. It was a bad dream.

On the doorstep was another handwritten envelope. Opening it with shaking hands, she felt like an idiot –

it was an invitation to a drinks thing at the clubhouse.

'Shall we go?' she asked Jonathan, as they forked through the rib of beef, pan fried potatoes, green salad with Maria's own honey and mustard dressing. He made a face.

'I hate all that small talk about vacations and artisan cheese. "We bought this delicious cheese in the market here, you can't get it at home" etc., bloody etc. For Christ's sake, there's nothing you can't get in Manhattan. And I only like vacations where I still work. Which no one else does.'

You make enough fuss about oat crackers and Brie, don't you?

'We'll go for ten minutes if you want to – might make you feel better. I know you love to dress up. You are feeling better, aren't you? You look better.'

She dressed, as always, carefully – a black low-cut linen dress that was both smart and cool. Some pearls. Small pearl ear clips. A tiny black velvet clutch. Black low-heeled sandals. Soft red lipstick – Chanel.

There was a buzz of conversation at the clubhouse, but not the roars of laughter and hysterical giggles she'd expected. In fact, it was subdued. She couldn't see Fiona and George.

Jonathan asked the barman, 'How ya doing?' – his all-purpose greeting.

'Not so good, sir,' the barman said. 'There's been a tragic accident – one of the guests' children.'

'How is the kid?'

'It was a fatal accident, sir. Drowning.'

'How could that happen? The ocean's so shallow at the beach... How old?'

'Ten years. He swam out too far. Another Scotch?'

A drowning – especially of a child – wasn't good for business. Or was it? Fiona and George weren't there. Emma knew they'd never be there again.

'Jonathan, I think I know that child. The parents. I met... on the beach.'

'Emma, don't cry. How well did you know them? You never said anything about them. Are you sure?'

'Of course I'm damn well sure. I saw the kids on the beach near me and talked to the parents.'

'It might not be the same child. It's terrible news, but you really didn't know them. Try to relax, Em... here's a handkerchief.'

'Other women are crying!' she gasped – but that wasn't true. Most people were drinking, talking, seeming to almost relish this piece of terrible news.

She glimpsed Fiona once over the next three days – wearing black, getting into a car that had parked near the clubhouse. George was with her, and the other two children. It was the day before the funeral. Emma walked to her favorite beach bar for lunch and could hear other guests talking about the death. The Spencers were driving back to their home, holding the funeral there, the tiny coffin following behind them.

Maria tried to talk about it, but Emma changed the subject. She tried to divert her. Finally, she had to say, 'Maria, I'd rather we didn't discuss it. It's too sad. What are you planning for dinner tonight?'

Maria didn't like this.

'No, but it is dreadful, Mrs. Bowden. The water here isn't dangerous! And how come no one in the family was keeping an eye on him? If you ask me, it's all a bit funny. Tonight? I thought grilled lamb and green salad followed by a chocolate and ginger ice-cream. I've made the ice cream myself,' she added, sadly.

'Perfect,' said Emma, just as sadly.

With two weeks to go before they returned to Manhattan, her mood fell lower. The accident. Was it... some way... her fault? Something she'd said? Yet she couldn't remember what she'd said, exactly. There'd been a fuss over kids burying themselves on the beach and then a nasty letter from them – did she shout at them again?

'Don't keep brooding on it, Emma,' said Jonathan. 'It's really nothing to do with you – it's a dreadful, random accident. Try to enjoy the rest of the break. We're going back soon, for God's sake.'

Of course, she hadn't told him everything – only that she'd met them.

Her sleep was sometimes heavy, but always filled with dreams. She was in a huge hotel, but had forgotten her room number. She was going from floor to floor, trying to remember it – going up and down in elevators, running upstairs, along corridors.

Hello? Hello? Emma, is that you?

The giggling, clear voice. There in the room with her.

'Jonathan! Help me!' she screamed, but no words came out.

Emma! It's only me... Hello? Are you there, Emma?

*

She woke sweating. Jonathan wasn't there. Pulling on a robe, she managed to get to the kitchen, where he was drinking coffee and reading work documents.

'Couldn't sleep – felt I could get through some of this damned admin,' he said. Then: 'Emma, for God's sake what's wrong? You look awful... did you have a nightmare? Let me get you a brandy.'

She sat down and started to cry. 'Could we go back early? Please, Jonathan. I'm sleeping so badly here. I keep... hearing things.'

'If you're "hearing things" it may be because you take too damned many of those sleeping pills. Reduce – "taper down" – from halves. Try to start quartering them. They can give you hallucinations. Come on, old girl, pull yourself together. We'll go back if you insist. But there's only another week to go.'

She insisted.

MANHATTAN, 1963

Back in their Manhattan apartment a few months after the vacation, she wandered around, looking at the rugs, the paintings (including a real Picasso), shelves crammed with books, working fireplaces and displays of hand-painted china plates. The comfort. The colors.

A roof terrace – big enough to sit out on – sixteen floors above the city. A basement swimming pool. There was a ground floor bistro if they couldn't be bothered to go out. Yes, she was a lucky woman. And gradually she started to relax.

'You know, I think I might be able to start writing again – I have an idea for a novel,' she told Jonathan over veal Milanese and pasta in an Italian restaurant they both loved.

'That's great, Emma,' he said, looking worried. 'You really think you're up to it?'

'Yes, I do!' she snapped.

'How about that sleep problem?'

'It's a lot better now. I'm walking around the city an hour a day – it helps.'

'As long as you don't overdo it.'

She woke the next day feeling happy and energized. Depression could lift, she knew. She was better at last! When the phone rang, she answered cheerfully.

'Emma?' said a male voice.

Her heart sank.

She remembered George. His child had drowned while they were staying in the same resort.

'It's George Spencer. I hope you don't mind my calling you... I tracked you down through the club at The Hamptons. We met there.'

They shouldn't have given out my number, she thought angrily. *They had no right.*

'Yes? How are you both?'

'Oh, alright... you know. It's been grim.' His voice cracked. 'We wondered if we could meet. We live only a few blocks away. Near MoMA. Would that be possible?'

'Yes, of course. Is there some way I can help?'

'That's what we were wondering. Fiona's become very depressed. She blames herself, though the kids have always been responsible and that beach is so safe and secure. It seems even the lifeguards never saw him.' His voice cracked again.

'It's a mystery, yes,' she said coolly, then added, 'I am sorry, really. Of course, we can meet, if I can help at all...'

They made an arrangement, for the next morning.

She chose a pale charcoal dress with a matching jacket, a double strand of pearls, and a charcoal clutch with a pearl clasp. She sprayed herself with Chanel's Number 22. With her new blond bob, she thought she looked pretty.

Fiona looked ten years older.

'I'm sorry,' whispered Emma. 'This must be an awful time for you...'

Fiona didn't try to smile or respond.

George bought coffee for them all. He still looked much the same except for dark shadows beneath his eyes.

'Emma, thanks for showing up,' he began. 'This is pretty difficult to say. Of course, the police investigated Joe's death but they put it down to misadventure, plain drowning, going out much too far. No one saw him go in and no one's at fault. There were other kids in the water, lots of them, younger than him – he was a good swimmer. He won a prize at school...'

His voice became husky, choked up. He coughed and started again.

'We remembered you a few weeks after the funeral... there was some problem with the kids? Didn't you speak to them the day he drowned? We're only trying to find some explanation, reason... of course, there may be none.'

Emma said, 'I... thought they were burying each other in the sand, but was mistaken. That's when I saw you in the club.'

Fiona looked at her bitterly. 'You shouted at my kids! You accused them of sending you a threatening letter! You upset Joe and that's why he... drowned...'

She was crying and her voice was raised.

'No, Fiona,' said George. 'All I'm asking Emma is... was there anyone else there when you last spoke to the children? They can't remember. Louise and James can't remember, I mean,' he added.

'I'm... not sure. I don't think so. But I can't be sure. Maybe... no, I don't think there was.'

'This is a waste of time, she's just a waste of time!'

George said an awkward goodbye.

Emma went to a department store and bought novels and an expensive notebook, then Chanel body cream and a new soft red lipstick. She had lunch, with two glasses of Sancerre, on the roof of a hotel. Jonathan called her when she got home, saying he'd be back late. Stretching out on the sofa, she closed her eyes.

Hello? Hello? Emma? I'm back! Hahaha! Hello?

The voice receded. With shaking hands, she phoned her therapist.

'I think it may be stress, Emma, but it's worth coming in. I have an hour tomorrow morning.'

She phoned Jonathan. 'I'll be home soon. I'll leave now,' he said. 'I think you've been overdoing it, as I said and as I warned. But, Em, please don't be so hard on yourself. The past, it's over now. Try and enjoy your life, Emma.'

She put the phone down.

She'd been following the therapist's advice – more exercise. It was an effort – it always was – to haul herself out of bed so early. Seven-thirty. She hated getting up. Yet after a shower, a mist of Chanel, pulling on new black tights and a tunic top, hair washed, she felt... OK.

The club was only a few blocks away. Expensive, but, 'Worth it, Emma!' Jonathan told her. 'Exercise is better than Equanil. Pendlebury says it and I agree. You'll be a new woman. All you've got to do is get up and get there.'

He made it sound so easy.

A gentle keep fit class wasn't exactly "exercise", but after an hour of "stretching" she did feel better. In the bar, as usual, she ordered something called a "breakfast energizer" – peanut butter, a banana and chocolate milk whizzed up in a blender.

'Exactly the wrong things for you – all fattening and addictive. You'll keep ordering more and more of them,' Jonathan had said in a satisfied tone, quickly adding, 'But have them if you enjoy them.'

Of course, he was right – she sometimes had a second energizer straight away and even thought of ordering a "double", though she doubted they'd have a glass big enough.

A few people sat in the café area. One seemed familiar – where had they met? Had they met? She associated him with something... unenjoyable, difficult... the beach.

'Emma? I thought it was you... how are you? Mind if I join you for a minute?'

His voice was not bright, not cheerful, yet she recognized some animation at seeing her. George Spencer.

'Have you been a member long? Not bad, is it? I'm trying to swim before I get to the office – of course I don't manage it every day, but you can have breakfast here. Wakes you up, you know...'

He seemed less confident; thinner, older. Still as good looking, though. George – father of the child who drowned at their vacation resort. He talked on in platitudes, until she had to say: 'How is Fiona? And the children?'

'The kids are fine, I have a good nanny for them. She's English. She does the housekeeping too. Fiona, well... she's been rather ill. Joe's death... She's in a private hospital – under very good care, of course. I try to see her every few days – they think it's best if I don't go every day.'

Not shocked, she said gently, 'Is she getting better?'

'Takes time. She's under a lot of medication. Of course, it's a beautiful place – huge gardens, a butterfly sanctuary, spa – she couldn't be anywhere nicer.' His voice cracked.

'How long has she been there?'

'A couple of weeks.' He said it as though he was apologizing.

'And the kids?'

'They're OK – I think they've adapted; I suppose kids do. They love the nanny – she's kind, not young, you know – more like a grandma. Very practical, a good cook. We're all well looked after – I don't have a thing to do in the apartment except pay the damned bills!'

With this, she understood he was lonely and bored and sad – but most of all, lonely.

They had coffee together twice at the club, and then, hesitantly, he asked if she'd have time for a lunch.

'I always feel so much better when I've seen you, Emma!' he said. Even that time at the beach, she'd found him attractive – when they were talking about the letter she believed had come from his children. Although he'd told her he was a lawyer, she sensed he wasn't a high-achieving lawyer – he worked in municipal law or conveyancing, she guessed. Though he clearly earned well, he didn't have that commitment, that passion for his work Jonathan had. She guessed he was more interested in his family, in relaxing and having a comfortable time. Fiona was – had once been – an excellent cook and housekeeper and didn't have her own career. He'd told her that. She guessed he washed his car every weekend. And he was fascinated that she was a writer – repeating that he'd "dabbled" but "never had anything published".

In which case, you're not a writer, she thought. He believed his writing could be helped by reading a good guide book. She suggested Lajos Egri's *The Art of Dramatic Writing* as a great "how-to" to start with – but its literary, careful advice wasn't the kind of "how-to" he recognized.

As they got to know each other, she often found it enough simply to watch his face – he was dark, with sharp cheekbones, long eyelashes (he said he had Spanish blood), and beautiful enough to be an actor. The pain he was going through only made him look more exquisite – the shadows beneath the still-bright but sad eyes, the weight he'd lost making him look younger, the air of unspoken pain and vulnerability more intriguing than that of the affable guy she'd first met.

She loved to see him lope into a restaurant or bar – he was six feet plus. In fact, it was enough just to admire his looks. It was worth the lunch to do this. Unlike Jonathan, he seemed incapable of talking about abstract ideas, being ironic, discarding clichés and stereotypes.

And unlike Jonathan, he was new to her.

Beginning a friendship – or relationship – in what were tragic circumstances added its own piquancy. It was as though they were doing something experimental, dangerous.

'And not enough people experiment with their own lives, hardly anyone,' Emma told him after one champagne-fueled fish lunch in SoHo.

These were the sort of views he never heard from Fiona, he said, who talked – had talked – mainly of the children: dentist appointments, school triumphs, niggling worries she had about their future careers, the apartment, new furnishings they needed, what color did he think was right for the kitchen? They had to have the best, was her view.

Emma – and Jonathan – loved ideas. She would expound on hers, which weren't always fully planned out, while Jonathan watched and listened carefully and sometimes quizzically, always coming up with a more logical and intelligent assessment.

'The statistics show there are "only" three deaths a year on school trips,' she told George. 'Only three! There should be none – how can they admit "only" three in this casual way? In my view the school adventure trip serves no purpose – kids just go for a good time, fool around and get into serious trouble because they're "supervised" by moron teachers who don't take the care that parents would. How does it help your career to say you've spent a week in the Rockies, camping and cooking inedible beans over an open fire? They'll always refer to "bonding" – with school buddies half of whom you dislike or hate and mostly you'll never lay eyes on again.'

She had views like this on most things concerned with kids' safety. George seemed fascinated by her fluency, her interest in education, and of course her vast knowledge of books. Emma read at least four books – fiction, biographies, collections of letters – every week, and had done since she was a student. She disliked anything "contemporary" or "cozy", anything labeled romantic fiction, historical fiction, or airport reading. She ordered rare and vintage books.

'When do you get time to read so much?' George asked.

With some shame, she realized his life was bound up with Fiona's illness, his two surviving children, his job, worry and pain.

'Oh, when Jonathan works late – and it's really part of my job to read as much as I can. Unless you read widely, you can't be a writer. But it's different for you – you have so many worries. I'm so sorry, George. You didn't deserve this.'

For the first time she stretched out her hand over the crisp line of that linen tablecloth at The Russian Tea Room. He put his hand on top of hers. Some barrier had been crossed. They removed their hands, but kept them close.

They weren't embarrassed. Emma was excited. She didn't feel guilty. She was experimenting with life.

This first part – the lunches, the excitement of meeting, shows, concerts to dress up for – the first part was always the best part. Could she hang on to that?

When George made a reservation at The Algonquin, she loved getting ready. As she brushed powder the color of pale toast on to her cheekbones, outlined her lips and glossed over them the warm red lipstick, brushed her blond hair until it snapped and crackled, she was also thinking. Of the marvelous sauce they did with the shrimp at Delmonico's, the mouth-watering duck with orange and apple sauce at one restaurant, the fresh raspberry tart with English clotted cream at another. *We'll be having that soon*, she thought. *It's so delicious. And – I can have anything I want on the menu!* Of course, she could do that with Jonathan, but they always had the same things – veal Milanese for her, steak for him.

Jonathan rarely had time for lunch; surgeons didn't take long lunches. He hardly spent more than ten minutes on a canteen sandwich, he said. Which is why he liked having dinner at home, and didn't mind if it was a bought-in dinner – an expensive one, of course. And, while she read and listened to music, he'd go into his office and work again, often until midnight.

It suited her, because she was a big reader, though perhaps... lately she'd become lonely and, of course, there were periodic depressions. But – she absolutely loved having lunch and dinner out.

All the bits of her life worked. Didn't they? She'd told Jonathan she sometimes saw George, but he was unsurprised. 'A man in his position will grasp at a situation which links him with his loss – it's not unusual. Enjoy yourself, Em. I'm glad to see you back to your old self.'

George was engaging, but, after the novelty wore off, not interesting. He was sentimental. He tended to talk in clichés. He didn't read much, despite all his book talk. Lunch and movies were ideal; there were visual and oral pleasures to savor. His idea of "a good book... a story well told" was Dickens or John Updike – both brilliant in their own ways, but... She liked sitting opposite him in a restaurant, especially enjoyed the food, but after a few months, she enjoyed it all less, except the food. She began to feel the familiar restlessness, the depression.

She'd lost interest in the idea of going to bed with him – she saw the dangers there all too easily – but he seemed to think this might still be on the horizon.

'We will have a weekend together some day, won't we?' he pleaded. 'I miss you when I get home. It's just the kids to talk to, and the nanny... I'm not saying we could ever be a long-term thing – wouldn't presume to – but Emma, I am in love with you. Very much.'

She knew he still visited Fiona, who was unchanged. When she saw him after the visits, he looked haggard, didn't say much, needed her to hold him, stroke his forehead. These were the times when she felt she did love him. She knew, though, this wasn't really true. Just a feeling. A fantasy. They continued on: shows, cinema, meals, drinks in dark, candlelit bars – her favorite.

He said one day, 'When Fiona gets better, I guess we'd... for her sake... you know...'

'Of course! We could still have lunch now and then,' Emma agreed.

'But for now, let's make the most of it. You know I love you.'

From this, she guessed he didn't expect Fiona to get better. Was counting on it, in fact.

Though she didn't over-encourage him, George had decided to write about his lost son. He wouldn't give up on his idea of writing "Joe's story". He mentioned it every time they met. He showed her notes he'd written, all much too sentimental.

You're making Joe out to be a saint! she thought, but said, 'He was a normal little boy – wasn't he cheeky and naughty sometimes?'

'Never,' said George. 'He was the perfect boy. We never had a moment's worry with him. You should ask Fiona.'

Emma said gently, 'How is Fiona? Now?'

'Not better, but not worse.'

'What... does she do... during the day?'

'They paint and draw. Do yoga. Listen to music. She has her own shrink, and sees him most days. But she's on medication... it makes her sleepy.'

Fiona's routine sounded familiar. *But then I had a future ahead of me. Does Fiona have that?*

Now they talked more about Joe's story than about their relationship, Emma was tiring of it. Was feeling low again.

Loosening his tie and lying back on the couch, Jonathan tried to keep his voice even.

'I have a long day in surgery. It can be punishing – not so much during surgery, after. When I get home, I need a Scotch, a decent dinner, pleasant conversation, a calm atmosphere... we have a daily maid, for Christ's sake! But I get home and sometimes she's crying, depressed – she's still in her gown, maybe even still in bed... it's always about her career having gone down the drain... what can I say? What can I do about it? Even if she'd let me know, I could have ordered something in – I don't want to eat downstairs on my own. Now she even hears voices. Christ. She takes too many pills, is why.'

'She sees a therapist?'

'Pendlebury.'

'I know him. Good man. Jonathan, I think you need to be patient. You and Emma... a long marriage, good times... think in practical terms. Could your maid stay and serve dinner, for example?'

'Emma doesn't like maids to see her depressed and in her pajamas at dinner time. She likes them to leave at four. Then she gets depressed.'

'I see. How's it affecting your work?'

'As I said, it's not affecting it. I'm a surgeon. I have to focus – you know that. It's when I'm not at work – I'm starting to feel depressed too. Oh, she has good days and bad days. More good days lately. But I never know what day it'll be for her...'

'You know, many men go through this with their wives – I have three clients in the same situation right now. Successful women, working in media mainly, now with their work going through the floor... depression often follows. Don't do anything drastic. Patience is the key.'

The therapist accepted Jonathan's $200. An appointment was made for the following week.

Jonathan went straight into the nearest comfortable-looking bar.

'Scotch. Double.' He launched into the bowl of nuts, even though they were fattening and unhealthy and had been on the counter for days and he'd said he'd never have bar snacks again.

'Em, you're not unhappy. You think you are. Be patient and things will get better. You'll be published again. You have that new contract, remember? It's just a question of getting down to it. Working. Not giving in to depression.'

It was true her agent had accepted a submission for a novel – a kind of diary of a housewife struggling to cope with the demands of husband, children, lover and her own dark thoughts. But she had problems getting started. Some days she stared blankly at her typewriter. Could she deliver on what she'd outlined to Eve, her agent? She thought not. She'd had a few short stories published in magazines in the past, of course, but this... was harder.

She was still in her robe, but her hair was brushed and she had a little lipstick on. They were holding glasses of wine.

'I'll order in some Thai – what would you like?' he offered.

'I'm not hungry. I'll have some of yours. Order what you want.'

He reached out for the phone. He ordered.

'You'll feel better with food. What have you had today?'

'Pretzels. A banana.'

'If you don't eat, you will feel depressed. It's on its way. I'll lay the table.'

'Thank you. It's so dark out there.'

Jonathan came home one evening looking anxious. Emma happened to be up, dressed in black trousers and a pink linen shirt. She'd seen George for lunch. She had supper ready – she'd phoned for it ahead – a tomato and basil soup, a dish of duck salad, and a lemon cheesecake.

'Things are looking up,' said Jonathan as he sipped – or gulped – a Chablis.

'Yes, I'm feeling better,' she lied.

'Em, remember that anonymous letter you had while we were at The Hamptons? The one you thought was... from those kids on the beach?'

She nodded.

'The police called me today. That letter was from Maria, the maid. I was never sure you liked her. Wasn't she a bit difficult at times? Anyway, they'd been doing some investigations into staff there and she admitted it. I imagine she got scared. She's had treatment for depression. They said did we want to press charges? I said I'd ask you.'

She sipped. Thought. She felt better, genuinely – it was something new to think about.

'No, I don't. It's over now. Guest maids feel jealous of us... they do all the work. I never felt comfortable asking her to do things.'

Jonathan looked relieved.

'I guessed that's what you'd say.'

'And I was in a bad mood then, often… I… snapped at those kids…'

'Let's forget that now. You've nothing to blame yourself for. At least that's one mystery cleared up. And you're feeling better – you've got this new project to work on. Haven't you?'

'That's right. Things are looking up.'

'You know I'm a liability lawyer, don't you?'

George's words interfered with her tasting the silky Béarnaise sauce.

'No, I didn't know. Are you?'

'I was going through some old precedents – we mostly deal in school and work accidents – and saw – forgive me, Emma – that you'd been involved in a school accident.'

'Why are you saying this? It was years ago. No one was blamed. It was an accident! How dare you mention it?'

'Don't get upset. It's – you don't see me so often now, don't return my calls. I depend on you. I can't live without you.'

Don't be so hysterical.

'Are you saying you'd blackmail me?' Her voice became hard and high. 'You can't. That information is secret.'

'It's not "secret" if it's leaked to the press. How would it look – an author who accidentally killed a child? Not great publicity for you, is it? You've even written children's stories in the past.'

'I thought you loved me!'

'I do. Love you. It's because of that – I don't want to lose you. Can't live without you.'

She saw that perhaps Joe's death, Fiona's illness, their affair had driven him into some cul de sac of madness. Or paranoia. She had to get out.

'I'm leaving now, George. I can't bear to hear you talk like this – and can't bear to be reminded of... things. Thanks for the lunch.'

Leaving him staring after her.

She sent Eve, her agent, a note telling her about the accident on the cliff and saying she'd understand if they didn't want her on their list. She figured it was simpler to do that than wait in dread for George to say something – if he ever did. Anyway, it was easier to be the one to "own up" to the past.

Two days later, Eve called and asked her to lunch.

She guessed – she'd tell her with regret they'd have to pull the new novel. Cancel the contract.

An author who'd killed another child while on a school trip? Even accidentally, it didn't look good. And the parents would certainly welcome an opportunity to blame her again. Everything she'd tried to forget would be re-hashed.

She didn't taste the first course of the lunch – though it was her favorite, shrimp cocktail. The agent talked gently, sympathetically – Emma told her of the quarrel, her spiteful push, the sickening shock when the girl skidded over the cliff. And the six months in the children's unit.

'But, Emma,' said the agent, 'I'm not denying the pain this has all caused you, but with the right treatment this – incorporated into your novel and your marketing – could be excellent. Everyone feels blame, feels they are to blame for dreadful things they did as children. I once pushed a girl into a hedge of stinging nettles – she fell in face down and cried, the pain must have been searing, and I laughed at her, because I hated her. I still feel bad about it, to this day. What you did was a tragic extension of that. Can you envisage using it in the diary novel? I know it would resonate with readers. But I understand if it's too – difficult. And you'd be writing fiction, not a personal account. Ignore this guy's attempt to blackmail you – it's meaningless.'

Emma accepted a second glass of Pouilly-Fuissé. And actually tasted it.

'It might... work,' she said.

MARRIAGE

She'd always been a writer. At Vassar, Emma had sold her first short story to the *Saturday Evening Post*. She'd based it on a train journey she'd had in France, a strange young man sitting next to her, and as the night wore on, they chatted to each other. He was American, too. Then, in the small hours, she fell asleep with her head on his shoulder. Once in Paris, they took a taxi to a hotel, where they made love passionately and perversely. Then, waking to what she'd done – they'd done – she said goodbye.

He said, 'I serve you,' putting his hand over his heart, kissing her goodbye gently.

She knew they'd never meet again. And the way they met and their rapid embrace – you couldn't live like that. It was a wonderful fantasy she'd been lucky enough to live out. But it was always her benchmark for romance. Even marrying Jonathan didn't live up to that night.

After their wedding at The Plaza in New York, she and Jonathan left for Paris – her idea – by ship. Art and love – and food – everything was perfect. Everything. To be an American in Paris – the ideal. She trawled happily round the art galleries, they lunched on the Left Bank, got up early to go around the flower market at sunrise. Spent hours in The Shakespeare Bookshop, even went to a poetry reading there. This was their happiest time – and always would be. She somehow knew that.

Yet it was during their honeymoon she first snapped at Jonathan – simply because he said he didn't like to try cold mushrooms in oil and vinegar. Once she'd snapped, she felt pain – her first harsh word to him and just because he'd grumbled about a French dish. In every respect he deferred to her, looked after her, paid for her, and always made sure she was warm enough, cool enough; that their table was quiet enough, light enough, dark enough; that the wine was exactly the sort she loved best; that she rested, saw the films she wanted to, went to the plays she wanted to. Listened to the concerts she wanted to. He couldn't have been kinder – and there she was, snapping at him.

'Oh, for God's sake. It's one of the great French dishes. Don't try it then. See if I care.'

He'd looked hurt – seeing the desperate look on her face – but smiled and said, 'You're right. I really should try it. But perhaps not today.'

Wasn't it better not to have closeness and intimacy when it was at such risk, and you felt so terrible when you transgressed the "happy" line? When you knew you could never, never go back to that pre-first-harsh-word, those palmy days of finding no fault with the other? Once the first harsh word has been said, when will it stop?

It won't stop. It's the great lie. That you'll be happy ever after.

*

But they were, still, happy. Hand in hand, they walked across Paris, north to south, east to west. Saw everything they wanted to see. Ate in bistros and brasseries. Went to European movies. She'd taken some classic Capri pants and little jackets, linen dresses in bright, clear colors... but in Paris she bought a leather jacket, fitted, from a market stall. How different she looked.

'You look great,' said Jonathan.

'You know, at Vassar I never had a leather jacket – or a denim one. I wore cashmere twin sets, jeans and pearls or expensive silk scarves. I had a fur coat – the kind you could throw over you or onto a seat and never worry about making creases. I loved that fur.'

'Where is it now?'

'I sent a picture of myself wearing it to Mother. She wrote back saying she loved it too and she'd never had a fur – probably never would have. I felt so bad, I mailed it to her as a gift. You see, I didn't deserve it.'

'Rubbish!' he said heartily. 'You deserve everything. But it was generous of you to send her the coat. It was a kind thing to do. Boy, am I getting peckish! Where would you like to eat? That kind of workmen's lunch place you loved – or somewhere smarter, more Left Bank?'

She felt much less stressed away from New York. There were just as many cars hooting, you had to hang onto your purse everywhere, the sidewalk cafés were crowded... but no skyscrapers. No danger of falling bodies here. All the women were beautiful and thin and well-groomed – the men too. Perhaps she'd book into a beauty parlor tomorrow and have a manicure. Beautiful things and beautiful people. *That's what I love best. And my work.*

'Let's go to Versailles tomorrow,' she said.

MANHATTAN, 1964

She's stopped seeing George. She's feeling worse again. A lot worse. It's a mixture of fear and depression, but mainly fear. She has something to be afraid of.

She droops over a coffee in a department store, tears pricking her eyes, wishing she still had some kind of ordinary job, despite its boredom. Working from home on her new novel – she's quickly become lonely and despondent. It isn't going well.

She's tried the odd bookstore job over the last few years – a lot of fiddling with tills. Deadly. She couldn't get used to not being important. She's even tried office work – which was easier to do and even had a kind of Zen-like endurance about it – but before too long, it became ghastly too. But now, anything to put her mind elsewhere – anything to stop the tick-tick-ticking of anxiety. She wakes up to anxiety, and goes to sleep – when she does sleep – with anxiety. Of course, there is, could be, a remedy... one she'd prefer not to think about.

Her period is thirteen days late. She slept with George – didn't she? She did. She must have done. And it is never late. And, this time, it could only be George. She and Jonathan rarely sleep together now – she prefers her own bed, uninterrupted sleep, and he likes to work late. It's comfortable. She keeps checking every half hour but... nothing.

She wanders into a bookstore. Something gripping to read, something to take her mind off it.

She finds a paperback of short stories by Elizabeth Bowen – one of her favorite writers. At Barnes & Noble, she chooses a book, looks at a few pages, then puts it in the crook of her arm and "reads" her way to the door, stopping to browse other books on the way.

She thought of what she was doing as a magazine article on shoplifting:

1. As long as you look confident, display (don't try to conceal!) your stolen goods and move steadily to the door.
2. Don't rush.
3. Even open the book and stand or sit reading it. Read your way to the door!

That morning, she's already lifted a couple of magazines from a newsstand, and foundation testers from a drugstore. Those were easy, really – the magazines went under her arm and would look as though they were free; the testers she slipped into the pocket of her coat. Who cared about cosmetic testers left to dry out and crumble on the shelf?

She would never talk to anyone, not even her therapist, about her shoplifting. Why should she? She never felt guilty. But she'd rather no one knew. She deserved free magazines and books. That was all. And big shops accounted for shoplifting, so she wasn't stealing from real people. Everyone knew that.

Saturday morning. She lay in for a while, knowing she had all the time in the world. But by mid-afternoon, her spirits sank. No period. By four o'clock she was in the bookstore, a new novel in hand, preparing to add it to her bookshelf.

Someone tapped her on the shoulder.

Her heart really did seem to stop.

She turned to face a cheerful young man with a clipboard.

'I'm doing a survey on book-buying habits, madam,' he said. 'Would you have a few minutes to answer some questions? How often you shop here, how you decide what to buy, and so on?'

'Of course!' Breezily she responded to all his silly questions, making up most of the answers. Her heart was still hammering. After he'd finished, she looked round the store a bit more. When a fresh group of Saturday shoppers surged in, she drifted out. Walking quickly away, she felt lighter, refreshed. Adrenaline was pumping. And at the same time, familiar cramps were starting up... the relief! If it was... it must be. Had to be.

The book was in her bag. She went into the nearest smart ladies' room, and checked all was well. And all was well – she never needed to see George again. Never again. She and Jonathan could enjoy themselves. She'd cook interesting dinners every night, find a different club, get up early every day and work on her novel. Anything was possible. Anything. It was a fresh start. In fact – had she ever slept with George? Was it… some kind… of phantom feeling? Didn't Elizabeth the First's sister, Queen Mary, have a phantom pregnancy? To do with her anxiety. Of course. But it was over now.

She began to make a list.

And she started – really started – on her novel. At last.

George phoned one morning when she was happily going through recipe books, planning a dinner at home with two of their oldest friends. She'd canceled an appointment with her therapist – she didn't feel she needed it – and instead made an appointment with her hairdresser for that afternoon. Her writing was going well.

'George.' She tried to make her voice cheerful, noncommittal. 'I'm sorry I haven't returned your call – I'm working on a new book. My agent's already placed it. How are you?'

'You haven't returned four calls,' he said. 'And before that I saw you less and less. Emma, have you gone off me?'

'At the moment… I need some space. I need to concentrate. I'll be in touch… later.'

'I don't think you will,' he said.

MANHATTAN, 1965-1966

The novel is nearly completed. That night, half way between sleeping and waking, Emma was angry again with the Spencer children. Furious. Emma was furious with the Spencer children for lying about her. She'd told their mother they were burying each other in the sand – a dangerous game – and they'd said she lied. Then they sent her an impudent anonymous letter calling her selfish and wicked. But she'd seen them.

'We were supposed to be on vacation,' she told herself. She was as angry as if the incident had happened that day, not months ago. Years ago? And – her fury was as fresh. Her memory – was it clear?

After leaving the parents in the clubhouse, she saw the three children playing on the beach. She went up to them.

'I know it was you who sent me that dreadful letter,' she said. 'How dare you?' She moved closer. 'I want an apology – now.'

Scared, they clung together.

'It wasn't us,' said the one called Joe. 'You've got it wrong. I'm going to tell Mom and Dad. Or the police.'

'The police? They'd be on my side! I was trying to stop you from harming each other! You could have died, little brats. You are bad children.'

He ran off, crying.

She left them and walked to a beach restaurant. She was shaking. It wasn't the first time she'd told strangers' children off. The way mothers treated their children! She'd once seen two of them gossiping while their kids tried to feed a huge swan that had stepped out of the water. Its sharp beak – the fact that swans were aggressive – what could they be thinking?

'Swans are dangerous – don't let your children near them,' she'd said.

They weren't pleased.

Kids ran wild around department stores, bumping into things – only a few months ago a child had died when a fitment fell on him. And the parents were nowhere near.

'Please stop your child from running wild here – there are lots of dangers,' she said to people, and, 'You must hold your child's hand on the escalator!'

Sometimes they thought she worked for the store, but always they were resentful. One even said, 'What's it to do with you, lady?'

She never saw any mothers taking what she considered real care of their kids. Often the mothers were too engrossed in shopping. Always they were with other mothers, weighed down with strollers, carrier bags, cans of drinks – and non-stop chat. The kids were pacified with expensive toys in expensive shops. There was never any question of kids being told to pay attention, to take care, to keep their voices down or not to run around.

Emma tried not to read all the news, but the horror stories were compelling. Children, left to wander, were led away by child molesters – sometimes murdered. No one had seemed to warn them never to speak to strangers; they had no inbuilt sense of danger. Children fell into zoo enclosures of gorillas or lions, while their feckless mothers screamed and crowds gathered, not wanting to miss the horror. Some even took photographs. Children drowned in baths, in paddling pools, in garden swimming pools. They ran out of their own homes in their underwear – and were found dead a week later. Meanwhile, their families arranged what were really begging campaigns for "search costs" and gave endless extravagant tributes and interviews. Most of these searches incorporated a "vigil", with attendants asked to bring their own candles. Funerals – also funded by campaigns – meant coffins lavishly decorated with TV characters.

Don't think about it, Emma told herself. She recognized her anger was excessive. She feared her own anger. She knew it was something to do with the accident. By rebuking all these mothers, was she trying to compensate for her own horrific action? Hadn't she done the worst thing, the very worst thing, in the world – and gotten away with it? Why didn't she feel sorry for others, feel compassion? She had no answer. Her therapist had helped, but not in the way she thought. She felt more serene after she'd seen the shrink – and during – and for the next day or two. But was it a temporary camouflage? The guilt and pain never went away. Sometimes she forgot it for a while. Especially when she was in love.

But that didn't last, either.

Her anger with those Spencer children – had it been too extreme? She remembered one running away, crying – she thought he'd run to his parents. Which he had, apparently. Yes, that's what he'd done.

It was only hours later that he was fished out of the ocean, lifeless.

Warmed by her agent's encouragement, Emma set to on the finishing touches to her new novel. And now her agent knew about the accident, it didn't matter what George said. She put him off when he called to ask her out. He stopped calling. In any case, as a lawyer he'd be acting illegally to release any private data – but perhaps that fact hadn't escaped him.

She stopped reading news, which seemed horrific – the tortured children; the wives murdered and left in bin bags; the drunks wandering into rivers; the climbers dying on mountains; the tourists eaten by wolves.

She worked every day in the morning, finding it easy to get up at seven and go to her desk. It never crossed her mind to shoplift anymore. And that was one thing she left out of her press releases – she just wrote that she'd thought about it when she was depressed. Thought about it, that's all. Possibly, most women have thought about it. She didn't have to admit everything.

She finished the novel.

The first press releases about her new book – which mentioned Emma accidentally killing another child when she was ten – provoked a flurry of requests for interviews, pictures. These Emma found surprisingly easy. She concealed nothing. At least, that's how she saw it. She accused no one.

'No, I've never got over it – and I've always felt guilty.'

'Therapy can help in the short-term, but it isn't a solution. There isn't one.'

'Yes, I was adopted at eight years old. I already felt like a bad person then – despite everyone's efforts to welcome me. If you're adopted at that age, there's always damage. If there's a remedy – it's work. It stops you from over thinking, may give you a sense of achievement. The unit I was sent to encouraged me to write – I'll always be grateful for that. My husband has been endlessly patient.'

Hundreds of readers wrote in to say they'd felt the same – and to thank her for making them feel normal, see they could deal with the pain. There were TV interviews, and briefly she hosted a local chat show for adults who'd been adopted; another for adults "sent away" when they were children. There were complaints as well – from therapists, from parents of adopted children, from people who didn't agree with her views. But the letters of approval far exceeded the complaints.

Her biggest event was at a church hall in Brooklyn; several hundred people bought tickets. She was to read from her book, *Manhattan Diary* – a preview reading. Then answer questions. Then sign books. People cheered and clapped when she walked on stage. She was a celebrity. No more reading for free in small bookshops.

She spotted George and Fiona sitting unsmiling near the front. They didn't come up to have their book signed – had they even bought a copy? The line was long. She smiled and chatted to everyone, and signed her name and dedicated books in their name. Jonathan was with her, but seemed to have disappeared.

When the signing was over, it was time for a glass of wine. Where was Jonathan?

She saw the three of them, together, talking and laughing.

When she joined them, she saw Fiona's face. It was radiant. She looked twenty years younger.

She told Emma she was expecting a new baby. And it was nearly three years since Joe drowned.

'Em, you're doing so well now – your discipline is great. I'm so proud of you – think you'd be up to hosting a little dinner party here? Just two other couples – two guys who it's useful for me to entertain. You know. Sort of celebrate your book?'

'What are their wives like?'

'Oh, the sort of women men keep pictures of on their desks to cover their backs. Homely. One's a nurse.'

Besides their own maid, Carla, she hired two maids to spring clean the apartment and shine everything that could be shined – so she had gleaming cutlery, sparkling wine glasses. Buckets of flowers, all pink and blue – hydrangeas, geraniums, roses, freesias. The rugs were deep cleaned and returned as fresh as new. Jonathan ordered a crate of the best wines, red and white, and French champagne. She picked out a pale blue antique dinner service they'd had for ages and never used – and a linen table cloth in palest pink, and hand sewn, with matching napkins. The slim, tall candles were pale blue. She laid a fire in their working fireplace – and saw their beautiful room come to life, like a Bonnard painting.

What to give them? After ages going through recipe books, she decided on a lobster cocktail; a roast of lamb seasoned with garlic, rosemary and lemon; her home-made mint sauce; fresh peas and sweet potato fritters. She followed this with a creamy cake decorated with wild flowers, vanilla frosting, and a chocolate and peanut butter sauce. Oysters on the half shell to start.

Jonathan moved around the table, topping up glasses, and after the first awkward introductions and when the drinks had hit, talk was lively. Both wives seemed to get canned quickly, laughing too much, while the men were more moderate, talking some sarcastic shop, skewering their boss's judgement, questioning latest research in medicine, Jonathan joining in with their wives' laughter.

Emma, in her favorite low-cut black shift dress, confident she was the most attractive woman there, and also the one with the career, expected the wives would talk to her a lot, kind of... defer to her. But no one mentioned her books, and mostly they talked kids and homes.

'That new Miele dishwasher – a star! As good as having an extra maid in your kitchen. I don't know what I'd do without it. We have a simply marvelous new coffee-maker as well...'

'This dessert is gorgeous. Did you make it yourself?'

'Not exactly... I made the sauce. It's melted rum truffle with cream and a little peanut butter. Where are you going on vacation this year?' Emma asked sweetly.

'Paris! I can't wait to see the Left Bank, the flea markets. They say the cheese is out of this world. The artisan cheeses. The fresh vegetables. The kids can't wait either: Tommy does French at school, though he's only nine. Even if I say it myself, he's bright for his age.'

And they were off again... kids and vacations.

She usually took a sliver of a pill to help her through these evenings – and these pills did help. She was Emma Bowden, vivacious, smart, witty.

When they'd gone – thank God! – she took a slug of bourbon and another sliver of Equanil. She thought about what she'd done on the beach. It seemed a long time ago. Didn't Fiona say it was three years? She remembered shouting at those kids – twice. They'd sent a letter – or had they? Didn't Jonathan say it was from Maria, their maid there? She didn't go back to see the kids. She didn't chase Joe into the sea, surely? Though she'd have liked to.

Dishwashers, coffee-makers... the bore of it! She liked talking about new films, ideas, books. Once or twice, Jonathan had exchanged an, "I'm sorry! I know you can put up with it! It'll be over soon!" glance at her, and she'd smiled back, indicating a need for a refill.

George had once said about Fiona: 'On an intellectual level, we don't have much in common. She wanted a big family, so did I. She likes cooking, housekeeping, you know. She does like reading. But she's not like you.'

Nobody's like me.

1931

She remembers how her real mother smacked her because she, at five, wouldn't get into the bath. Skidding naked on the wet floor, she fell and cried. Her mother, shocked, started crying too and together they wept.

In the kitchen was a bottle of bleach, she knew it could make someone sick, so sick they would die. She poured some into a glass, and added orange juice.

'Drink, Mommy... feel better,' she whispered.

Just at the last moment – as her mother was about to sip it – she snatched the drink away and ran into the kitchen, throwing it in the sink.

'No, Mommy!' she gasped. 'Wrong drink!'

Yet a small smile appeared on her mother's face – she must have smelled it, known it wasn't just orange juice – and they were friends again, clinging to each other. Among the piles of unwashed clothes, rubbish, empty food boxes on the floor. That's how they lived – in a permanent rubbish tip. What did that matter? Mommy loved her, she knew.

When she was fostered and then adopted, she'd cry herself to sleep sometimes.

'Mommy! Come and get me! Oh, Mommy..,'

She told her adopted mother (who she never called

Mommy) one winter's night, 'When I'm asleep, I fly to Mommy... even through the cold and snow.'

When she was given dolls, she made them talk to each other – conversations she could remember.

'"Why'd you let her go, Suse? Why'd you let her go?"'

'"I can't manage her. I can't manage any of them. It's too much, it's too hard!"'

Girls at her new school taunted, 'Your real mommy gave you away.'

MANHATTAN, 1966

A few months after the boring dinner, she and Jonathan were invited to a party at the home of a TV scriptwriter. An apartment with a pool right outside the terrace. A butler serving miniature lobster canapes, tiny squares of caviar on toast, finger-sized coffee eclairs, little cubes of iced birthday cake, each with a sugar rosebud on... with tall flutes of French champagne.

A celebration party in Manhattan. Crowds of screeching people, a room too small to hold them all, loud music, hysterical laughter... drugs? Girls with wild curly hair to their waist, wearing kaftans and rows of beads... rumors that Diana Dors would turn up... "drop in", anyway... a feverish atmosphere.

But, as it turned out, there was nothing to celebrate.

Two days later, Emma had a visit from a couple of police officers: one tall, dark, like someone from a Visconti film; the other, small, chubby and nervous. The tall one did most of the talking.

'I'm sorry, Mrs. Bowden – no doubt you're still shocked. As you know, a two-year-old girl, Sophie, child of one of the guests, drowned in the pool. We're told the child simply "got away"' (he put inverted commas round the words) from her parents and was later found in the water. You were on the guest list, and we're seeing everyone who was on it. Did you see the child?'

'I saw her at the start, yes, with her parents. But it was a huge party – I didn't see her after that, though I saw her mother and father. I assumed she was with her nanny.'

'She had no nanny with her. So, you didn't play with the little girl? Or see anyone with her?'

'No. I didn't. I didn't know her.'

The Italian-looking one stared round the room, then said softly, 'Mrs. Bowden, I believe you were at The Hamptons when Joe Spencer drowned?'

Her heart began to thump.

'Yes, we were.'

'The parents said that at the time, the children annoyed you in some way?'

'They sent me an unpleasant note, yes, or at least I thought it was from them. I can't pretend I wasn't angry.'

'Yes. Do you still see the Spencers?'

'I've seen George, sometimes, as we go to the same fitness club. Fiona, no. She's been ill.'

She'd forgotten Fiona had recovered.

'Is that a real Picasso?' He sounded admiring.

'Yes, it is.'

'Nice. We may need to see you again.'

He looked again appraisingly at the Picasso.

When they left, she burst into tears.

'Jonathan! They think I killed Sophie!'

'Get a grip, Emma. They're interviewing everyone on the guest list – they have to do that, for God's sake, and your name was there. The Joe Spencer thing was a coincidence. His drowning was random; they said so at the time.'

She still shook and cried.

'In any case – in *any* case – that child was shockingly looked after. Rich parents, probably had a few drinks, can't even keep an eye on their own little girl. In a mad crush like that she could easily get lost and wander off to the pool. If they weren't taking care of her.'

'The terrace leads right on to it,' she said. 'A little girl would just walk into it... simply step in.'

'Em, a brandy?'

She recalled the evening. Loud rock music – The Rolling Stones – deafening. She'd retreated to the bathroom, feeling jittery. Claustrophobia and loud music, two of her favorite fears – the levels were alarming. She planned to move to the terrace when she came out – it could be done. Desperate, she hadn't any pills in her evening bag. Oh, the cool air! The bright blue of the water... too blue. Not like real water... not like real sea.

And that's when she heard screaming, saw a blur dive into the water, heard alarm sirens. Paramedics, sweating, shouldered their way in and tried to bring the child back to life. The mother was screaming, weeping, throwing herself onto the child. They were taken to hospital. Everywhere she could hear hysterical cries of "She's dead! She's drowned!" Everyone was asked to leave. She and Jonathan left, sat on their own terrace with large drinks.

The horror of the scene brought its own post-horror adrenalin – it was almost peaceful. All Jonathan said, quietly, was, 'A totally unnecessary death. Most deaths I see in this city are.'

All Emma could think was, I was in the bathroom then – I had to get out. To the terrace. That's when it happened...

Don't think any more, she told herself. Sleep.

The good-looking Italian one dropped by again.

'We have a suspect for the death of Sophie – but we need more evidence,' he says, lounging on the sofa, wearing shoes a little too pointed for a cop. 'You say you were in the main room, and then you went out onto the terrace? Can you recall what you saw?'

'I wasn't feeling well. A little claustrophobic – the music was loud, the room was stuffy... I was desperate for some air.'

'Was anyone on the terrace at that time?'

'I... don't think so... maybe, yes. I don't know.'

She recalls having said these words somewhere else, another time.

'Please think hard, Mrs. Bowden. It will help us.'

She thinks.

'I had the impression of... a blur. Something red.'

'The child was wearing a red dress.'

'And then, I think... someone else dived in, there was a splash. And then crowds of people screaming.'

'The person who dived in, can you remember what they were wearing? Even the color? A man or a woman, would you say?'

'Maybe, black... perhaps... a woman... I can't remember clearly.'

'When this person dived, you were the only person there?'

'I think so. But of course, I can't be sure. There may have been someone behind me, I don't know. I can't imagine I was the only one feeling claustrophobic.'

He says she's been helpful, takes another look at the Picasso, chats for a few minutes about modern art, then leaves.

A week later, the child's mother was arrested. Suffering from depression, she'd pushed the child in and then tried to rescue her. Her husband had tried to cover up, insisting she'd dived in after the child, to save her. The mother was a fashion designer: glamorous, often on television. Her husband was desperate to protect her. Emma heard on the grapevine that, when his wife was arrested, he begged the police to arrest him instead, to let him take the blame.

As always, Jonathan was calm, measured. 'She was a brain disabled child – they had to take her everywhere with them, she wouldn't let them go out without her. She had no regard for safety and wandered off – I guess the mother was temporarily out of her mind. She pushed her in, then instantly regretted it – but it was too late. A brain disability – when the child looks fine, is pretty – is hard for parents to deal with. But the mother could have gotten better treatment.'

Emma could understand why she'd pushed the child in, but not why she'd tried to rescue her.

'Jonathan... is there something wrong with me? I feel more sympathy for the mother than for the child. I'm absolutely sure I could never cope with a brain damaged child – every day would be torture... you do see that?'

He saw. But added, 'People do cope, and with far worse. The human being can be infinitely compassionate. The thing is, never to judge. I still think the child could have been more carefully watched. But I imagine the mother was enjoying herself for the first time in ages. She was very depressed, but alcohol and a party atmosphere can temporarily uplift. I did judge them then, but didn't know the child was brain damaged.'

'She won't be put in jail, will she?'

'I'm sure not. They'll advise some medical help. It's enough for them to live with it. That's enough of a punishment. Yet they will recover.'

'How do you know?'

'I don't "know". But there's always hope.'

MANHATTAN, 1967

Her novel *Manhattan Diary* continues to be a great hit. It's on bestseller lists. It's translated into nineteen languages. Critics recognize her stressed heroine, Carol, struggling to cope with apartment, children and difficult husband, panic attacks.

All women will recognize some of Carol's problems, and many women, all of them, writes one critic.

She's asked to write a piece for the *Saturday Evening Post* on being a student at Vassar in its all-women days. She recalls long evenings – nights – spent with her best friends Ruth and Mia, the conversations, the comfort of it. The pleasure. They'd stayed friends. They always would.

Being all-women was much better, she believes. She makes an argument for it, written in her witty "diary" style.

She accepts all publicity: her agent advises it.

'All publicity is good, Emma. Bite the bullet!'

The make-up girl uses all kinds of cosmetics Emma hasn't tried, contours her face, blow dries her hair, sprays some shine onto it, suggests a different, softer but still red, lipstick. She's forty now – on TV she looks ten years younger. Make-up – what would she do without it?

*

She was being interviewed again for television, following her Vassar piece, this time on the rise in student deaths by suicide. It was because her *Manhattan Diary* novel was haunted by "falling bodies" – two characters jumped from balconies. She'd said that, walking in Manhattan, she was always wary of the falling body, the person falling from a great height. Worse, she knew that opposite her own building – her own building! – a diplomat's wife threw first her two children, then herself, from the twelfth floor. She was suffering from loneliness and depression, the inquest recorded. After that, a "welcome group" for diplomatic wives was set up. Then, visiting a friend in hospital, she was told that the friend was sitting on the window ledge smoking when an old man flung himself from four floors above her. She witnessed the blur of his falling body. Her friend began to cry and became anxious.

The nurses said, 'He was old and going to die anyway. Please don't think about it anymore – concentrate on getting well.'

So callous! She'd always found nurses to be cool and rather heartless – maybe that was too drastic an adjective, maybe not – while male doctors had more… sensitivity. Seemed to anyway. Their voices were better modulated.

To throw oneself from a great height… it would be painless, she thought.

You'd lose consciousness before you hit the ground.

And there would be the thrill of flying... and seeing everything, albeit for the last time, from the air.

The TV studio, early in the morning, was a little chaotic, almost domestic. Coffee was offered, jokes made, the presenter read through notes in a panicky but show-off last minute way. Then "insider" jokes were cracked between the team, who clearly felt themselves a cut above everyone else. The slot began with the latest student suicide figures – getting higher each year. Every university had at least one suicide a year, some three or four. Yet there had always been suicides at Vassar. Emma knew – she'd researched it ahead of the TV show.

She quoted from a newspaper report of 1925 – Miss Anna Bailey, twenty-one, hanged herself in her room with a scarf attached to her clothes press. Her poems "showed ability" though she was subject to "fits of depression" and the coroner concluded there was "no adequate reason" for Miss Bailey to hang herself: "Temporary insanity was responsible".

No "adequate" reason? What would be an "adequate" reason?

Another Vassar girl, the daughter of a priest, drowned herself in a water cistern at her home because she felt she wasn't doing well enough – that she'd let her family down.

Yet another, a film major, set fire to herself.

'Of course, Jackie Kennedy went to Vassar – around your time; and there were suicides then.'

'Philosophical suicides,' said Emma.

'What does that mean?'

'Two girls, brilliant philosophy students, did commit suicide when I was there, but they'd always been fascinated by death. They were always talking about it. To them it was the great adventure, the great mystery – they had this theory that, if one was going to die anyway, why wait until you were old and ill and hopeless to do it? Why not do it when you were young and could, as they said, "enjoy the journey?" They were discovered in a weekend studio they rented, both in black silk nightdresses, with their arms around each other. Medicals revealed they'd taken huge overdoses of a sedative drug which first induces euphoria. Their notes said goodbye and thank you to their families, and that they'd embarked on what they called, "The most fascinating journey of our lives – we're on a thrilling voyage. Don't mourn for us".'

'What did staff and students make of that?'

'There was grief and sadness mixed with... a kind of puzzlement. Women at Vassar were thinkers – there wasn't a clichéd reaction. No one wrote "RIP" anywhere, or "Heaven has found a new angel". We'd find that absurd. With some students, there was almost a kind of awe.'

'Awe?'

'Some students were impressed they'd taken their beliefs so far. Hadn't backed out. In fact, a sort of group, a cult, was set up to look into death and death writings. I don't know if it still exists. I left in 1947.'

'Do you remember the girls?'

'Yes. I do. Kelly, and Mary Lou. Both blond, slim and pretty. They were tremendous dancers – they did an exhibition rock 'n' roll, and a perfect tango at dances. It was great to watch them.'

'Was there a backlash to this tragedy?'

'Some parents took their daughters away from Vassar. There were complaints to the principal, and the trustees were involved. Then there were tabloid accusations of "black magic" and of course suggestions that drugs were a serious problem. There were drugs. Plus – boys were not admitted at that time, it was an all-girl college. That made life so much easier – there was little or no anxiety. You could relax, come to class without make-up, never worry about whether a boy liked you or didn't. I believe admitting boys to Vassar was a mistake. It's so much easier to concentrate on your studies without also being embroiled in a romance. When boys are at a college, a kind of hierarchy sets in – who's the prettiest girl, who dresses best, who has the most boys like her? It's so competitive. Then, when a relationship goes wrong – and you still have to see the boy every day – life would become misery to the girl. It's enough to study – then relax with your girlfriends. No wonder there's so much stress and anxiety at college now! No woman student should have to put up with dealing with men as well.'

'Apart from the professors, you mean?' However, the interviewer said this, smiling, with the microphone off. And that was the interview done.

The double suicide was a faint memory.

After all, they'd talked about it so much! The "afterlife" – whole groups sat up late into the night discussing it. Which Emma thought was stupid. The death-groupies talked endlessly about what might happen, how we'd all have to die. How curious death was and how little curiosity was shown.

Suicide? They thought it a fascinating option. A bit like doing the *Caminito del Ray* walk near Malaga – a hair-raising walk above steep gorges and falls, with just a rope to hang on to. Something she'd thought she might attempt for the terror – but knew she never would. At the same time – and only now and then – she could see it was a tempting option. Death. Or endless sleep, which was the same but without the inconvenience for everyone else.

Her *Diary* book is still doing well – in the USA and in Britain, as well as other countries. She's doing notes for another one, based on a woman's relationship with her shrink. She's working at her best.

One day her publisher had a note for her. The handwriting was untidy, in pencil. The signature – who was it from? She saw "Cathy". Cathy who?

Cathy! Her sister – the sister she never imagined she'd see again:

> *I saw your book in the Book store here, with your Picture on it. We live in Omaha where we have a nice trailer and not so far from the river. Wayne and me have 5 kids, the baby is only 3 months old. Our brother – Mikey – he died years ago when he was 20, a bike accident, I'm sorry to tell you this.*

It would be nice to see you, if you ever could get here. The camp is signposted and there's a motel not far. The book looked good, though I couldn't buy a copy then. I hope to though.

A blurry snapshot was enclosed. Cathy looked overweight, her partner thin and undernourished, the children all smiling and making silly faces. Emma didn't feel a thing. Except surprise. All those years when she'd felt the pain of losing little Cathy – and now to be confronted with this huge woman... she raked her emotion for some shred of feeling, of affection, attachment.

She felt much sadder when she thought of Mikey dying in a motorbike accident. Tears came into her eyes. Didn't they meet in New York? About seventeen years ago? When she was working in a bookstore? As always, she appealed to Jonathan for advice.

'Should I go to visit? She is my sister. But that trailer... and she's huge. Yet why should that matter so much? Why aren't I kinder?'

'You aren't unkind, Em. Obesity is off-putting. I imagine the family lives mostly on trashy food. It may be difficult to cook in that trailer. I think you have to consider responsibility rather than emotion here. But remember Cathy has chosen this life, chosen to have five kids. Wasn't she adopted, too?'

'Yes. She was. We all were. But the addresses weren't shared. We lost touch. It looks as though... she hasn't done well. She looks like my natural mother. She was overweight, too.'

She found she didn't want to visit, couldn't face it. 'But I could send a check. I could ask when the children's birthdays are.'

'Yes – that would be a great idea. It's a good thing to try and help them in some way – even though they haven't asked for help. Unless you feel you'd really like to see her.'

'I've seen enough,' she said.

She wrote a warm note, enclosed a check, asked for the names of the children and their birthdays, and said she'd hope to see them when she could make a visit to Omaha.

A note came back saying Cathy didn't have a checking account, and could Emma please send the money in cash? She was sorry for the trouble.

After putting the cash in a registered envelope, Emma felt better. At the same time, she was more curious. The first shock of the letter had passed. Cathy was her sister.

Omaha, 1969

She was working now on her new novel, the woman-and-shrink one, which she'd titled *The Shrink Who Needed Me,* managing to be up at six and at her desk soon after. But by lunchtime, she felt drained. It was essential to get out, but first she'd have a rest. Sleep. Sometimes so heavily she slept the afternoon away.

'It would be better to get some air, Em, when you've finished work. Then when you come back, sleep if you must. But I'm confident that if you go out for a walk, you won't feel so tired.'

She walked – and began to notice fat women. Even street people were obese. Some women were so overweight, they walked with sticks. Was Cathy one of these? Why was she living in a trailer? Didn't her adoptive parents bring her up well? And all those children – her nieces and nephews.

It must be so cold there in winter. *Is that place big enough for them all? What does Cathy's partner do?* In the picture, he looked so thin, he actually looked ill.

She asked Jonathan to study the picture.

'He is exceptionally thin and drawn. It could be drug use, or an illness – he may not be eating. I can't tell from this, but certainly he isn't well. I can't imagine the conditions there are healthy. It's best not to speculate. If we're able to see them – and if you feel up to it – we could drive down one weekend, and stay in a decent hotel to break the journey. Then find a place to stay, and drive out. There is some wonderful scenery around there.'

'Should we do that?'

'It's up to you.'

Remembering his word "responsibility" and also recalling him saying it was the hardest thing to accept, she thought they'd go. And she was now curious, as well as dreading it. She sent a note giving a date when they could visit. Cathy's letter back was rather formal. *We will be pleased to see you both.* But it also gave directions for finding their home. She signed off *Yr loving sister, Cathy.* Two of the children had scrawled their names – Cliff and Stevie.

Emma was as nervous as she could be. She wore a black cotton dress and had packed some blue jeans and crisp white T-shirts. There were little gifts for the children – toys and candy.

'I know how nervous you are, Em.' By the time they got to Omaha, she had a headache. Their hotel was comfortable and smart. There were chocolates in their room, and a wine list.

They located the park home. It was a long trudge to Cathy's trailer. Emma found her heart pounding; Jonathan looked perfectly calm. The door was open and children were sitting on the steps. They jumped up.

'Ma! Ma! Emma's here!'

A huge woman in a limp floral smock eased herself out and smiled, holding out her arms. 'Emma! Is it really you?'

Hugging her, Emma smelled sweat and onions. Behind her, the thin man appeared, grinning, embarrassed. He spoke with a rough country accent.

'Howdy. Good to see y'all.'

The trailer was full of trash – a plastic bin filled with takeaway wrappers, another of dirty clothes, heaps of toys scattered about. They'd recently eaten burgers and fries – she could see their remains. They sat on the steps outside, in the sun, with mugs of tasteless coffee. Emma had given the kids their gifts; they were running around now, shrieking and eating the candy.

Conversation was not awkward – Cathy talked a lot – but not informatively. Cathy said she left home as soon as she could, and didn't get on with her adoptive parents.

'Too fancy – they had their own daughter and they were always comparing me with her. Like she could talk French and I couldn't, and they were always making her talk it.'

'What did you do when you left home?'

'I knew some people from school who had an old apartment – not much of a place, but it was OK – and they made room for me. I worked in a burger bar. Then I met Wayne and got pregnant... I was seventeen. We moved around a bit until Wayne lost his job, and then we found this place. We managed to buy it – my adoptive parents did give me some money when I had my first – and we get by. It's lovely here in the summer. You can see.'

'Do the children go to school?'

'The older two do – the school's not far away and other kids from the park go there. People are friendly. Wayne hasn't been so well.'

Now she was closer up, she saw the marks on his arms.

'Are you… recovering?' she asked.

'I go to rehab once a week,' he admitted. 'But I don't have much appetite. The medicine they give you takes it away.'

She felt sad for them: the start of some emotion.

'I'm sorry. I hope things will improve for you, Cathy. What I can do is send you some cash every now and then, and for the kids' birthdays. Wayne, do you have medical insurance?'

'No,' he admitted. 'We use the welfare health facility.'

'Suppose you let Jonathan and I take out medical insurance for you, so you could get better treatment – would that help?'

'I don't know,' he said. 'We'd rather have the cash, I figure.'

She'd seen a crate of empty bottles by the door.

They talked on. Thankfully she and Cathy never started a sentence with, "Do you remember?" But Cathy did mention Mikey.

'He found out where I lived. He needed somewhere to stay once and he stayed with us. He didn't like his adoptive parents either – he was a bit wild. He could play the guitar. Real well.' Cathy said she'd been to his funeral. 'We got flowers made in the shape of a guitar! And the coffin had musical notes painted on it. Real pretty.'

Mikey… so sweet. My baby. Didn't we…?

'Did his… adoptive parents… attend?'

'They came. They paid for the funeral, the flowers and everything. The lady was crying. I met her, I thought she was OK. I don't really know why he said he hated them.'

He hated them the same as I hated mine – yet it wasn't their fault. No one wants to be adopted, that's all. No one.

'So… are you busy here?'

'Sure. I keep house, look after the kids and Wayne, get food – we have food stamps, you know.'

'Do you have friends?'

'Most people here are friendly – you get one or two who are odd, don't move out of their trailers, shout at the kids. But mostly it's a nice neighborhood.'

It became difficult to think of anything more to say.

Cathy got a huge pizza ready and offered it round. Emma and Jonathan took tiny pieces while Cathy and the kids had most of it, cramming it into their mouths, swigging cola. There was also a huge cream cheesecake that tasted stale.

'This is delicious, Cathy – thanks so much,' Emma said.

Soon they prepared to leave, saying they "had to get to the hotel to check for a message from work", which Cathy seemed to accept.

'We'll come again of course,' said Emma, in relief, doubting they ever would. 'If you're ever in New York, would you call us?'

'Never been there in my life,' said Wayne. 'Don't forget about that cash, will you? We could really use it.'

She felt dislike for him, longed to say to Cathy, 'What did you see in him? Why have you turned your life into something resembling our mother's?' But she could see no reflection of the small girl she'd looked after on those long nights.

Instead, she asked, 'Do you remember when we were all together? That dog we had? We called him Spot.'

Because they'd had a little dog, kept on a string attached to the gate, but he ran off, leaving them crying. They had petted him and fed him. He was the first real pet they ever had – she didn't count the snakes her mother had kept in a glass tank. Emma grew up with the snakes, so she wasn't scared – but you couldn't pet them or stroke them.

When child psychologists had talked to her, trying to establish what feelings she had, one had said, 'How did you feel about losing Spot? How did you feel?'

Emma couldn't say anything except, 'I don't know,' but they kept on and on asking. Eventually she'd said, 'When he ran away, I missed him.'

The psychologist had actually sighed with relief. Emma knew now that some children in care were so harmed by what they'd been through that they had no conscience, and no compassion or empathy for others. Everything had been wiped from them: they were unable to feel. Some would end up as criminals or recluses or, she thought, highly successful businessmen.

'I'm so happy we made contact again – happy that you wrote me, Cathy. And I brought you a copy of the book – read it when you have a bored moment!'

Inside she'd written: *With love to my dear little sister Cathy, from Emma.*

George rang again, a few months later. Maybe he'd had a few drinks. He sounded emotional.

'You helped me come to terms with Joe's death, but all the lunches, dinners, those evenings we spent together didn't mean so much to you, did they? I understand. Of course.' He spoke sadly. Added, again, 'I understand, really. I'm more than glad I had that time with you. You're an exceptional woman. I'm sorry I mentioned the accident when you were a kid – forgive me. I'm a little ashamed. I guess I was still recovering then...'

Why couldn't men understand that it was possible to fall out of love with them? Men had been falling out of love with women for years... centuries. That note she'd had from a professor she'd adored at Vassar: *Goodbye. Regrets.* After they'd had a glorious affair and talked of a "trial honeymoon" on Bermuda – she accepted it. She wasn't thrilled about it, obviously, but there was no guarantee you wouldn't "go off" someone. You didn't think you were using them... at the time you weren't. It was never your intention to use them. It was your intention to have a glorious relationship that lasted for ever, just like the glossy magazine ads of romantic, well-dressed, slim, coiffed couples in their seventies enjoying a "retirement village", clinking champagne glasses, holding hands as they look out onto a communal garden with rose bushes and benches. When had she ever met anyone like that? Elderly couples she knew were cranky, got on each other's nerves, both wore beige trousers and old-fashioned tops and clearly "comfortable" shoes. They sat looking around hopelessly, silently, in parks. Older women living alone yes – they often dressed well, exercised, seemed to enjoy their lives. The bliss of an apartment to yourself! Allowing you to sleep whenever you wanted without having to explain why, to clean up the place and know that when you saw it again everything would be exactly as you'd neatly left it. But... you might get lonely. In the dark hours of the night.

Emotion, love, was a phase... it lasted as long as it lasted. Work was better. When there was work. Irony was better than sentiment. Her relationship with Jonathan – their familiar shared lexicon. She respected his intelligence, his brilliant career, his passion for hard work. His wealth. He was never floored by depression or anxiety. At least, he never seemed to be.

Strangely, even with the success of *Diary* she'd felt down, lost, after meeting Fiona that evening, hearing she was pregnant... then seeing Cathy's children, especially the sweet little one. She'd taken a snap of him and often looked at it. He was adorable. Was it her period beginning – that heavy feeling of being dragged down, feeling depressed? She'd never really started

George's baby (she recognized now that she'd imagined being pregnant, lots of women did, a "hysterical pregnancy" or whatever it was called?) – but did she want a baby anyway? She'd always thought having one was a retreat from living, progressing – a backward step. Stopping you from working, being a success. Your verbal skills would fall behind – you'd be talking to four-year-olds all day, all weekend. Kids who didn't read anything but babyish books, would hate museums, would only want to go to Disney films, and eat fish sticks. Your life would become regressive, repetitive, infantile.

Sixteen floors up. What would it take to jump? People jumped from windows in Manhattan every day. She was taking about a quarter or half an Equanil at least every day, sometimes more. But that was nothing – almost "nullative value", a phrase she'd picked up from Jonathan. A joke word doctors used between themselves when they prescribed placebos. Her work was going brilliantly. She'd get the new book in on deadline. But she felt so tired, so sad, when she woke up. So hard to get going.

'A cold shower, Emma – it's one of the secrets. Another is to get up as soon as you wake up – don't lie there indulging in the warmth. Yes, it takes discipline – but don't you need that for your career? Above all, Em, don't sabotage this comeback.' Jonathan's voice becoming firmer.

1974

Her latest book, *The Shrink Who Needed Me*, had terrible reviews. So different from the applause for *Diary*. No one had asked her to give a talk. She started to have bad days. And really bad days. Her memories – were they manageable? What had her therapist said?

'Don't think so much, Emma.'

One prestigious critic had even written, "Who cares?" suggesting her work was narcissistic and pointless. All about rich housewives swaying around New York hailing cabs. Getting therapy. Since then, she's been listless. Not even enough energy to get angry. Could she shop? She's feeling better today. Jonathan had suggested she went shopping for herself; some new clothes, cosmetics.

'You always liked to do that – shop, have lunch somewhere smart – I'll leave you some blank checks. Early birthday present.'

It's been a while since she bought clothes.

Showered, dressed in a plain linen dress, cream, with Jonathan's checks and some charge cards, and of course a couple of slivers of pills, she tries to walk through the park to the stores. But after five minutes she knows she can't do it – she's too tired. Swaying around New York. She retraces her steps and hails a cab.

In the first store she feels panic – she's immediately assaulted by a "personal shopper".

'I'd like – a couple of plain dresses for the summer, maybe some shoes to go with them,' she manages.

Sitting on a spiky chair in the dressing room. The saleswoman – covered with a thick poultice of make-up, a tight black dress not flattering her plump figure, an overpowering perfume, fake lashes – brings back an array of dresses in the smallest size. All floral, some with bits of lace on, the shoes too fiddly and fancy – nothing like the classic look she's always aimed for.

In a couple more stores, the same thing happens. No shop has plain, classic dresses – shiny, glittery dresses; dresses covered in roses and daisies; midi dresses; gingham dresses; mini skirted dresses, yes. After offering her these, the salesladies admit defeat, or just don't come back.

Emma breaks into a cold sweat – she hasn't had one of those for years... she remembers that a cold sweat doesn't last too long. She knows it's a form of nervous terror.

Wearily, she finds a smart café. Or should she have a cocktail? Somehow, she doesn't think it would go with the half pill she's just swallowed on an empty stomach. She orders coffee and a plain chicken sandwich. Of which she eats less than half.

'Emma! I thought it was you!'

It's George. George Spencer. He stares at her.

'You look so thin, Emma! I mean, you look great – but you've lost so much weight.'

Fuck you. 'Yes, I haven't... been well. Flu.'

'Can I buy you a drink?'

Accepting a tonic water, she pretends, 'Everything's fine. My second novel was out recently.'

'Yes, I saw the reviews. That's great!'

She hears that Fiona, the children and the new baby – Barnaby – almost eight years old – are all fine. That means... it's eight years since they met. Is it? It could easily have been last week. Where did that time go? Where is it now?

'Fiona's doing two days a week working in a bookstore – she loves it. I've never seen her happier.'

She can't take much more of this. She cannot believe she was once in love with him – enjoyed his company, loved to look at his face, which hasn't changed at all.

Draining the drink, she thanks him and lies, 'I'd love to stay longer, but I've arranged to meet up with a friend for a late lunch. Come and have a drink with us some time – bring... Barnaby with you.'

They both know this will never happen, but pretend it will, and part warmly.

Tears pricking her eyes, she wanders randomly, in and out of stores. How long is it since she felt that thrill of "falling in love" – that glowing anticipation, the increasing delicious terror as the hours drew nearer to meeting? Is it the menopause, or something else? Some failure of the senses, some running down of internal machinery, some... end game?

You're being ridiculous. There's nothing wrong with not finding him appealing any more – as I remember it, you got tired of him anyway. He really isn't very interesting. But he seems... alive. What happened to his son, Joe? Didn't he drown?

She has a vague memory of finding the boy annoying – but that's all.

She continues round the stores, finding their piped music maddening, the clash of perfumes suffocating, the robotic faces of the salesgirls hideous.

As she walked through the store, a salesgirl sprayed a too-sickly perfume on her. Another offered her a discount voucher for an in-store manicure. Seeing the girl's frighteningly long, too-shiny black-red nails, she shuddered. She tore up the voucher, dropped the pieces on the floor and walked on, leaving the salesgirl gaping after her.

'Madam! You look wonderful today!' An androgynous young man, wearing full make-up and a smart black suit, white shirt and tie, murmurs to her. Inevitably, she turns around. 'I love your hair!' he continues. 'And your skin is perfect. But I wonder – would you like to try our "miracle" skin cream, completely anti-ageing? It's made from marine oils. It's used by Jackie Kennedy... I mean Onassis.'

The price of the "miracle cream" is eye-watering. Yet there's something about it.

'Could I perhaps try a sample?' she whispers. Jackie Kennedy, she knows, has a whispery voice.

'I can give you a seven-day sample – and perhaps we could make an appointment for a trial using all our products? In a private cubicle, of course. The fee would come off any products you buy. You'll never regret this

– Mrs. Kennedy, I mean Onassis, certainly didn't. She's one of our most loyal clients.'

Now that Jack's dead? How can she even get up in the morning? How could she marry someone else?

'I was at Vassar with her,' she says.

'No! You weren't! I guessed there was something about you – you have that same sort of style, that indefinable chic…'

He was well into his pitch now. Glimpsing her face in the mirror – bags under her eyes, her skin pale, her neck beginning to sag because she's so thin – or so old – she gives up.

'I'll try it. Thank you so much. Goodbye.'

She senses his disappointment, but can't be bothered to care. She wants not to hear any more of his beguiling yet terrible words… how easy it is to be lured in by compliments!

She finds a café bar where most of the customers are women, packages at their feet. Some in pairs. Laughing and looking through their carrier bags, gloating over their stuff. But she's not as happy as she used to be, lunching by herself. Are people staring at her? She wishes she'd brought a book.

A glass of wine is now a must.

'We don't have the fresh tuna today, madam,' the waiter says, handing her the menu.

'What tuna? I never asked for it.'

'No, we don't have it, I said.'

'Maybe – some smoked salmon with a little salad? Please don't put any onion in it.'

'Of course.' He glides away.

She sips her wine. When did eating out by herself become less of a pleasure? More of an ordeal?

Afterwards, in the bookshop, they had no copies of her novels.

'We could order one for you – it'll take a couple of weeks. Maybe three. But we're not re-ordering for the shop.'

She doesn't ask why.

Too weary to walk home, she flags a cab. The driver is loquacious, complaining about the behavior of black people who walk across the road, in the way of the cab. One, she sees, has a white cane.

'I don't think she could see well – and New York traffic can be frightening,' she said.

'More likely the stick's a fake – they'll stop at nothing. I'd like to see segregation back – the worst thing this country ever did was stop it.'

'Would you put me off here?' she snaps.

'Thought you wanted West forty-ninth, lady.'

'I've changed my mind.'

She throws some bills at him; he swears, and drives off.

She was in front of an expensive hotel.

'I can get his number for you, madam,' the commissionaire says softly.

'No, all I want is... may I use your powder room?'

'Of course, madam.'

In the powder room, she throws up. This city is

unbearable unless you're at home. Preferably in your own bed.

Another cab, this time, thankfully, with a silent driver, gets her back to the apartment. Jonathan's there. Why is he home so early, looking... so worried? Why is he home?

'Em, sit down,' he says. 'I've had some bad news.'

His mother. Youthful at seventy-two, still "chipper", had died that day in an automobile accident.

'She and Dad had an argument before she drove to the store,' he says, his voice cracking. 'They were always bickering – it didn't mean anything. Either he forgot to empty the filter on the dishwasher or left some cigarette stubs in an ashtray. Forgot to water some plant. You know how house-proud she is. Was. They had a row, she drove off, and the next thing, Dad has a phone call from the cops...'

She knew how proud they were of him, the only son. How pleased they were when she and Jonathan married. How they sent her folksy gifts – embroidered tea towels and oriental porcelain which she never disliked, but never used. They were wealthy – his father had been a stockbroker – yet still their favorite entertainment was a "variety show" with a "big name" like Frank Sinatra or Tom Jones.

When she and Jonathan visited, they always put on a barbecue, Jonathan's father wearing tartan trousers, and an apron which said, "Chef and chief bottle washer". His mother piling huge, tasteless, unseasoned steaks and lamb chops on the coals, serving salads of limp lettuce, beetroot and potatoes in bottle mayonnaise. With this, they served champagne, never quite chilled enough, but adequate – Emma knew Jonathan would have preferred red wine.

Sometimes they'd invite hearty neighbors, who'd ask Emma about her "latest blockbuster", and then return to property prices and the terrible behavior of young people these days. Once they were fueled with drinks, there'd be a lot of silly jokes and, of course, nostalgia. They'd recall trudging to school – no being chauffeured by cars – and strict discipline – none of this rock and roll and drugs – and polite, deferential store assistants.

'You gave them a list and they'd pick out the goods for you. And everything tasted of something. Not like that supermarket pap.' Charming, gracious, Emma would listen and chat, though mainly listen. Jonathan's parents were popular. They loved to entertain.

'Dad's completely distraught – you can imagine. He's had heart problems before and this might make them worse. I'll have to go down now, Em.'

She could see how desperately sad he was, his face ashen. *It's such a terrible way to die.* Did she die instantly? She wanted to ask, but thought better of it.

'Jonathan, I'll come with you. You can't be on your own.'

'Would you, Em? I didn't want to ask, knowing you haven't been one hundred per cent yourself. But you'd help Dad, I know. And I guess there'll be a lot of... stuff... to arrange.'

She desperately didn't want to go. She knew she'd hate every minute. She loathed funerals. And she hadn't been devoted to his mother, though they'd always been cordial – his mother going out of her way to find gifts for Emma; when they came to New York, taking her out for lunch – 'Somewhere you recommend and like, Emma. Your busy life... you know all the best places. Don't worry at all about the cost, have anything you like on the menu. I've been looking forward to taking my lovely daughter-in-law out! With your wonderful books... I tell my neighbors, she's a novelist, my daughter-in-law. Are they impressed!'

She was pretty sure neither of them ever read her books, though they did buy them. They'd been kind to her. They knew her background – that she'd been in care, adopted, involved in a dreadful accident as a child – and they never asked a single question, never tried to make her feel awkward.

'Of course I'll come, Jonathan. I want to. I'll pack now.' She'd leave a note for Carla.

'Emma, you don't have to. But thank you.' With the grace so typical of him, he even asked, 'How did your shopping trip go? Get anything nice?'

'Fine – but it doesn't matter now. I'll be ready in ten minutes.'

Her weariness seemed to have vanished, replaced by a terrible curiosity and sadness.

'It'll be hot as hell in Florida,' Jonathan warned. 'But they do have the pool.'

*

They flew down (she took three Equanils; driving would take too long), saying little on the journey. Emma sometimes grasping Jonathan's hand. Jonathan's father greeted them with hugs and a soundless weeping. Jonathan cried too. Only Emma remained dry eyed.

The bottle of bourbon in the kitchen – inroads had been made into it, Emma saw.

'Emma, what will you have?' said Jonathan's father. 'Mom always has sherry, Campari and, of course, wine. Any of those suit you?'

'I'll have a glass of wine,' said Emma, stricken by the use of "Mom". 'But aren't you hungry? I could fix something.'

'One of the neighbors brought round a casserole; it needs reheating. And there's a pudding wrapped in foil. But not for me at the moment, thank you, Emma. Maybe later.'

She imagined their Manhattan neighbors calling round with their casseroles, their foil-wrapped parcels... what would be the point when you could have anything and everything delivered? But she supposed there was comfort in these offerings; there must be.

They were talking now about the funeral – a priest would drop by that evening. Emma dreaded that – and who to invite. Every so often Jonathan's father would hold back tears, or say, 'She was only seventy-two! Seventy-two, for heaven's sake! She was so fit, so active. She still went to yoga. Swam every day. She had years left, years. She had so many plans.'

Jonathan put his arm around his father's shoulders.

The priest did arrive – a solemn, dull looking man who seemed embarrassed. Neither of the couple were regular churchgoers, but they were in his neighborhood. He asked what kind of service would be required – something simple, said Jonathan's father – and if the late Mrs. Bowden had any favorite hymns or readings.

'Not hymns,' said Jonathan's father. 'But readings – that Shakespeare thing: full fathom five thy father lies. And she loved Walt Whitman – Come in From the Cold, I think it's called.'

For music, they decided on Bach fugues; Jonathan would do the readings.

Cremation or burial? Cremation, they agreed. At this Jonathan's father did cry, gulping, 'I'm sorry,' as tears slipped down his face. The priest left then. Patting him on the back and saying they could ring him any time. Any time at all. Don't hesitate.

The worst thing about the funeral wasn't the service. Emma looked down through most of it, was aware of Jonathan's tight face, and knew he was holding back tears. His readings were dignified. The guests were mostly elderly, plus a couple of children who looked round brightly as though they were at a party. No, the worse thing was the reception – lots of chatty people, alcohol, elderly people eating a surprising amount of the buffet with apparent relish. Several people told her they were "so sorry to meet you under these circumstances" and to "look after yourself" and one or two actually said Dora was in "a better place".

How on earth do you know that?

When the guests had finally left – some going through all the sympathy again at the door – the three of them sat on the terrace.

'Have a swim, Emma,' said Jonathan's father. 'We have the pool cleaned every week. I could make you a malted in the blender, if you like – after all that alcohol.'

A malted! *He sees me as a little girl.* 'No, not today. But I will use the pool, maybe tomorrow. Thank you.'

They sat in silence for a while. Then the two men began on memories.

'I'll never forget your first day at school. You were fine, but Mom was crying when she got back. Don't suppose you can remember that, son?'

'Not Mom crying, but the first day – yes. They gave us each a chocolate chip cookie.'

A few weeks later, her close Vassar friend, Ruth, also a writer, had her first baby. A month premature. And unexpected. Caught out at last, in middle-age. Yet surprisingly thrilled! She called Emma from her hospital bed.

'He's so cute,' her friend gasped, sounding as though she was laughing and crying at the same time.

'When did you have him?' Emma asked, willing up an excited voice.

'Last night – early morning! I slept a little, but now I'm too excited! Brad's just been in – didn't seem to know what to do or say. Emma, could you come in?'

'Of course. I can't wait! I'll get a cab right over.'

*

Picking up a huge bouquet of scented flowers at the corner florist, she hailed a cab. She'd seen Ruth often over the years – they used to have lunches together as "young marrieds" – but not lately. The two couples used to go out in a foursome, sometimes calling in at three Manhattan parties on the same night. They hadn't done that for years.

Why don't we go to three parties in a night anymore? she whined to herself, thinking she should be crawling on the floor like a Tennessee Williams heroine. Then laughed out loud.

'Something funny, lady?' the cab driver barked.

Today of all days, she had to get a miserable driver when New York was full of laugh-a-minute jokers.

'I'm visiting a friend who's had a baby,' she said.

'Right.'

'Have you any kids?' Something made her ask.

'Did have. They don't wanna see me no more.'

Too bad. Though she knew she'd over-tip him.

The hospital – smart, the lobby with soft sofas and discreet reception desks. The nurses in sparkling white and blue trouser suits directed her to Ruth's floor, where a more officious nurse was in charge.

'Mrs. Katz is seeing visitors, but only for another hour. She needs her rest.'

'Emma! You made it!'

Ruth wore full make-up, her skin glowing, her hair brushed and gleaming. Beside her a scrap of a thing, in a cot, snuffling gently. The room seemed full of flowers, soft toys, a huge basket of fruit tied with a silver ribbon.

'Thank you for these gorgeous flowers!'

Was there a catch in her voice?

'How are you feeling? He's fabulous!'

'Yes, isn't he? I don't know. Fine, except I keep bursting into tears!'

They both laughed.

'Baby blues. Can I hold him?'

Ruth lifted the scrap from his crib.

'Hold him, Emma. He's so light – yet so complete. I didn't expect him to be such a real person. Separate from us. It seems funny that he actually has his own cot.'

Laughing, Emma hugged the little thing. Hugged him closely. Squeezed him.

'I was hoping you'd be his godmother, Emma.'

'Of course! Love to...'

'Emma? Do you think I'll be a good mother? He's lovely, of course, but I want to get back to work before too long.' She sounded tearful again.

'Of course, you'll be brilliant! And you have help for him, don't you?'

'Yes – we've hired a nanny. She'll have to live in for a bit, which isn't ideal. He's awfully small, isn't he?'

'Babies are small,' said Emma, firmly.

'Yes – but he seems frail. Do you think he seems frail?'

'No. But I think you're a little frail. You only gave birth a few hours ago. You need to rest. When is Brad coming in again?'

'He's gone back to the office. He'll be here around six.' Ruth sighed. Lay back on the pillows, tears in her eyes.

'I'll sit with you while you drop off. Will they let me do that?'

'You can stay until they come in and check on us. Thank you, Emma. I can't understand this depressed feeling. It comes and goes.'

'I've had that all my life!' joked Emma. She sat while Ruth closed her eyes. She woke again when the nurses came in.

'Visitors to leave now,' ordered the nurse. 'You can come back tomorrow, of course. But it's important to call first.'

'You seem anxious,' said Jonathan at dinner.

'Will Ruth be OK?'

'Sure,' said Jonathan. 'All new mothers fluctuate between euphoria and crying. It's perfectly natural. Don't worry, Em.'

But when she called the next day, she was told the baby had some "breathing problems" and was now in an oxygen mask.

'Will he be alright? How's Ruth?'

'A fair number of babies suffer from this, and recover. Others do not. Your friend is, naturally, upset. That's really all I can say at the moment.'

She sent a card to the hospital and thought about calling Brad – but felt she'd be intruding.

'There's nothing he can say,' said Jonathan. 'Wait a day or two. I'm sure she'll call you when things look better.'

Ruth didn't call. A couple of days later Emma heard the baby had died – its lungs too immature to cope with the breathing problem. She was crying when Jonathan came home.

'It's terrible! So unfair!' she gasped. She thought of Cathy in her squalid trailer, five healthy kids wearing grubby clothes, cramming takeaway food into their mouths.

'Yes. Life's unfair,' he agreed. 'Childbirth is still a gamble – no matter how sophisticated medicine is. Yet they can probably have another child. It's not impossible. The chances of this happening a second time are remote. I'm sorry. I know how close you are. Remember all those parties the four of us used to go to? Don't cry, Emma.'

She wrote Ruth a letter, trying to avoid the clichés – saying she hoped she'd feel well again soon, and maybe they could go out together, even go on a weekend away, when she was home.

And she thought back to their summers at Vassar: everything in front of them at the successful start of their lives, not yet stepping into the future. How easy it was to sleep heavily, get up early or late, enjoy friendships, feel bright and engaged. How clear the air. How fresh.

There was no reply for weeks. She heard Ruth wasn't going out much, hadn't even gone back to her job on the magazine. Emma decided to take the risk of calling her, one afternoon.

'Emma! How good to hear from you.' Ruth sounded just the same – but Emma knew how a phone call from a friend could give a voice false energy. 'Come around! I'm feeling so much better.'

She called a cab round to their apartment. On the front door was a garland of white flowers. Ruth looked happy and smiling; the apartment fresh and pretty. They embraced, Emma with tears in her eyes.

'You haven't met our new little one.'

On the floor was a Moses basket. 'I made the patchwork quilt myself,' said Ruth. 'It's easy as you need so few squares.'

Astonished, Emma stared.

It was a doll.

'Come on, little one! Say hello to Auntie Em!'

She held the doll out to Emma. Emma tried to cuddle the "baby" and murmur something, but the situation was... but she didn't want to upset Ruth. Had a doctor or a shrink told her to use a toy as a substitute? How could Ruth be taken in by this sinister claptrap? An intelligent Vassar woman?

Ruth sat and cuddled the baby. 'She's on solids now,' she told Emma. 'You can get them in all kinds of flavors – chicken dinner, vegetables and ham. She likes the applesauce and apricot one best.' Emma couldn't stand it. Couldn't stand her friend being manipulated like this by some screwball shrink.

'Ruth, you do realize she's a doll – not a real baby, don't you?' she said gently. 'She can't eat or drink, or anything.'

'How dare you talk about my baby in that way? You – who've never even had a child – dare to criticize mine! Wait until I tell Brad you said these things! Get out, now!'

'I'm sorry!' Emma gasped. 'I didn't mean it – I was only trying to help.'

Ruth burst into tears. 'Get out before I call the super to throw you out!' she cried, clutching the doll to her.

Stunned, Emma left.

'I'll never see Ruth again. We'll never be able to get over this. We were best friends. Isn't she concerned about what people will think? They'll think she's nuts.'

'She is – temporarily – ill,' said Jonathan. 'But it's far better for her to grieve with a "baby substitute" than be trapped in a black tunnel of despair. There's a school of thought that believes just holding a doll helps her feel better, promotes happy feelings.'

'Like a kitten, you mean? Why not have a kitten?'

'Emma, I don't know. Perhaps they don't like cats. But it's not for us to judge. Anything that improves the quality of her life now is a good thing.'

'But does she realize it is a doll – it's not real?'

'On some level she'll recognize it. But the doll is making her happy right now. Helping her cope. That's surely better than her being in a hospital bed pumped with drugs.'

'She told me to get out!'

'In a while she won't remember that. You were attacking her fantasy, a fantasy making her feel so much better – it's dangerous. Like waking someone who's sleepwalking. It's not your fault. Though it would have been better if you hadn't said it. But don't worry about it now. Please.'

*

That night the voices came back – laughing, giggling, calling out to her. And she saw a doll with a vicious face, mouth open, laughing and calling out to her.

Eve phoned one day.

'You don't have to respond to this, Emma, but I had a letter from the brother of the little girl who had that tragic accident when you were small. It's a polite letter and he apologizes if it would bring back bad memories for you. His mother is now very ill and not expected to live long. She'd like to see you before she dies. Just to talk about Moira. I'll send you the letter, but only if you want me to. Please, Emma, don't do anything you don't want to do. Think about it first.'

She thought. And thought – why not? Wouldn't it be something generous to do, when her thoughts so often concerned herself? A woman at the doorway to death, could she help in some small way?

Jonathan approved of her decision, and said he'd drive her down.

'You may feel sad afterward, Em. I'd like to be there for you.'

But she preferred to take the train, knowing the long journey would be soothing. She could fly – but that would be stressful. She hadn't flown since the visit with Cathy, apart from the three-Equanil horror to the funeral.

The journey to Vermont was beautiful. Wonderful scenery, a long unfolding canvas of green. The first class had a waiter service – butlers with flutes of champagne;

langoustines with delicate fresh shrimp sauce, lime, grapes, and fig salad; roast Cornish game hen with herb stuffing, and tiny baked potatoes and spinach; a fresh chocolate fudge cake with dark chocolate icing. She had two new paperbacks to read – Elizabeth Bowen's *To the North* and a Patricia Highsmith she hadn't read before, *Strangers on a Train*.

She'd dressed carefully – a loose camel cashmere coat, black linen pants, a pale yellow shirt, shiny black ankle boots, a glossy leather bag half way between a briefcase and an overnight bag.

At the station, she called the son.

'So kind of you to come down – we really appreciate it. Would you be too tired to see Mom now? This is often her best time. When the light goes down. She has a room with a nice view. I can meet you at the reception there.'

Not feeling at all panicked, she made her way to the hospital – chaotic reception area and an elevator to the fifth floor. The son, Larry, welcomed her – a man with sad eyes. Thin, tired.

'She may not say too much and her voice is a little slurred – the drugs,' he explained. 'She hasn't got long to go. But she did want to see you.'

He opened the door and moved back into the corridor. Emma was aware of many sounds: a bleeping noise, the hum of a fan, the buzz of some machine, a far-off intercom, trolleys being wheeled. Smells... disinfectant, some light cologne thing, even coffee. The woman's harsh breathing, her body wrapped in sheets and wired up to several machines – she seemed already a corpse. But the machines were keeping her alive, just a little longer. Why?

She approached the bed, touched the figure lying there.

'I'm Emma, Moira's friend.'

The woman opened her eyes. 'Thank you for coming,' she managed. 'We often thought of you in hospital, so young.'

Emma's eyes filled with tears. 'I'm sorry,' she whispered. 'So sorry.'

On the windowsill was a photograph of Moira. She looked innocent, studious, friendly. How could she have hated this child? Such an open face.

'Not your fault,' the woman said. 'The authorities. Not you. Moira. Did she... when it...?'

Emma knew exactly what the question was. 'She was laughing,' said Emma. 'We were fooling around, having fun. She'd never have known a thing. I remember her laughing... she was one of the most popular girls in the class.'

There was silence. She saw tears slip down the woman's face.

'Moira was my good friend. We had lots of good times together.' That was all Emma could manage before her voice cracked. She reached for the woman's hand and held it, gently, because it was paper thin. She saw her eyes had closed. Emma stayed on for another ten minutes, then left. The son was waiting.

'Your mother's asleep now – we talked a little...' She felt exhausted.

'Would you like to come to our house and have a meal? My wife would love to meet you – she's seen you on TV.' She saw it would be a distraction for them – waiting for his mother to die would be... both agonizing and boring. But she couldn't manage it.

'Thank you so much, but I think I'll go to my hotel. I'm a little tired right now. But let me know if you'd like me to visit again in the morning – I'd be happy to do that. My train's in the afternoon, or I can get a later one.'

In the morning, he called her to say his mother had died "peacefully" (what did that mean, exactly?) during the night.

In her dream, she was falling, falling from a great height. There was a sense of, "It is really a dream, you will wake up", yet it was still frightening. Gasping, she jolted awake. And remembered.

'It's so funny, you think he likes you, but he's told Sylvia you look like a horse! Hahaha!'

Hatred seared though her. She wasn't sure how far away the cliff edge was, but she knew it was slippery. Her own boots were smeared with mud. It could be done. She snatched her hand away, and pushed – pushed as hard as she could – so Moira first skidded, then fell right to the cliff edge. Then rolled over to her death.

Emma didn't move. She planted her feet astride and stood hands on hips; she was glad – *glad, glad, glad* – she'd killed Moira. She'd got what she deserved. Then Emma started shaking. Screaming for help. Sinking into the mud, so she had to be hauled up when the rest of the group arrived, gathered round her while she sobbed.

'She slipped,' she kept gasping. 'She just slipped. I let go of her and she slipped.'

Then, in deep shock, she said nothing at all. Nothing when she was taken to hospital. When her parents arrived, she turned her face to the wall and kept her eyes shut. Mostly she was terrified she'd be sent to prison – what then? Her life would be over, she'd have been found out.

Lying in the hospital bed, she rarely thought about Moira's death. She thought about herself, how wicked she was, how people would know she was wicked – that was the worst bit. When they'd decided she'd go to a children's unit, there was a small sense of relief. Not prison, then. No one had blamed her for Moira's death. No one knew she'd done it deliberately. It was possible she could get away with it, could endure the children's unit, would one day be freed.

Her parents – did they know? They'd had to put up with a lot when she first came to live with them, after she'd been in care. The tantrums, her inability to relate to other children. Neighbors' small children came to play and she'd walk up behind them, pretending she had a huge spider in her hand.

'Why did you do that, Emma? Why?' shouted a little girl, while the other two children drew away from her. She accused one girl on a sleepover of keeping her awake by walking to and from bathroom.

'We'll have to cut off your feet so they don't make any noise,' she warned. The nine-year-old started to cry. She phoned her mother to ask to be collected early.

'I want to go home now and see Mommy,' she sobbed, while Emma's adoptive parents tried to calm her. Later they asked Emma not to say "cruel things", but Emma remembered much more cruel things said – and done – to her, before she went into care. Or rather... she tried to forget them.

Emma? Where are you? Emma! I'm coming to find you, Emma!

Sweating and shuddering, she jolted awake. Really awake this time.

She saw her shrink the next day.

'I believe this is stress again, Emma... stress and over-thinking. Are you taking any medications?' Dr. Pendlebury knew about self-medication and his patients – that was a given.

'I have... an occasional sleeping pill.'

'Do you take them during the day?' His voice was matter of fact.

'No! Of course not! Just... when I can't sleep. I half the 7.5 ones. Nembutals.'

'As Jonathan said, it would be better to wean yourself from them. He's an excellent doctor, and you should take his advice. They can make you think you're hearing things. If you're taking them every night, your system gets used to them and you have to take more and more.'

'The voices are so real! And it's always the same voice. A young girl, a child... laughing... I get so frightened... don't you think...?'

'What is it you want me to say, Emma?'

Defeated, she said nothing.

'How's your work going?'

'It was going well – my new novel is out. It's about therapy. But I had to make a visit to a dying friend, and haven't slept well since. I'm always tired during the day because I haven't slept.'

'Yes... my advice to you – prescription, if you will!' He laughed. 'Exercise. A few laps at the pool, a brisk walk around the city, even a dance class – all these are tools to help you feel better, stimulate your metabolism, and something else to think about. Could you go to an art class, draw or paint? You have an art history degree, I seem to remember.'

'I minored in it. I majored in creative writing.'

'Art is a therapy that gives an immediate gratification. I'm not sure writing does that – though if you feel inspired and can lose yourself in writing without worrying about the outcome, of course that's excellent. But I imagine it's rather a lonely occupation?'

'Yes. It is.'

'That's why a class of some kind will improve your mood. Even practical cookery is a good one. I say "even", because perhaps, with your background, it seems too ordinary. But it can be satisfying. A distraction will help those "nerves" of yours.' He laughed again.

'Thanks. I'll think about it.'

She scrambled off the couch, as desperate to get away as she'd been to arrive. Reaching in her purse for a check, which she'd already made out for the enormous sum Dr. Pendlebury required to tell her damn all that was useful.

'Don't think too much, Emma.'

Deliberately not making a new appointment, she left, shaking. Yet when she'd stopped shaking, a sense of well-being crept over her. It's the adrenalin, she told herself. He's a bastard – a bastard I depend on. It's a relief to get away. And yet she had the feeling she'd been "told off".

She booked a cookery class for the next day – a day "workshop" in "easy Italian cookery". You cooked three dishes and ate them at the school, with a glass of wine "provided" and a free apron with the school's logo on it. Oh, give it a try, she told herself. It's something new to think about. It's not Vassar, but it's something. She went to the class, but left half way through, running down the stairs, laughing. Her dish had burned while the others were all perfect.

1950

She'd done so well, on a scholarship to Vassar, that she managed to win a guest editorship at *Mademoiselle*. She found a one-room walk-up in Manhattan, with a tiny shower. She slept, cooked, and worked in her room – and loved it. Furnished lovingly with thrift-shop rugs, bright red enamel coffee pot, and plain white plates and jugs. She painted the walls white, her bedspread was faded patchwork, she used an old wooden table as her desk and always had a white jug with fresh flowers from the market.

Life was grand. New, unspoiled, rolled out just for her. She sent letters to her adoptive parents, but never considered going home – of course, they asked her. She never wanted to see... that place... again. Never.

Back then, if there had been one small problem in her fresh, intoxicating life, it was sleep. If she'd worked late, really late, she was able to come home and fall into bed, woken by her alarm, it seemed, five minutes later. But when she was home at a reasonable time, she went to bed around midnight. And then began to notice the street noises – cars revving, bikes squealing, doors slamming, people yelling or laughing, dust carts groaning, music from other apartments. She tried ear plugs, eye masks, even putting on her own quiet "yogic" music, but sometimes nothing would send her to sleep.

Tina, one of her friends, gave her a few of her own "precious" sleeping pills.

'What more friendship can a woman show than by giving her friend some of her own sleepers?' laughed Tina, warning, 'You have to go down on your knees to a doctor to get them.'

Which Emma wasn't prepared to do. She never wanted to see the inside of a clinic again – though, of course, she'd been "fixed up". Not pleasant, and she didn't always use the rubber thing they gave to her, but it was one of the chores you had to endure.

She was feeling elated and happy. She'd done a short story reading – a story from her Vassar thesis; a story that had already been bought by *Mademoiselle* – along with other young writers at a small Village bookshop. The evening had a college feel, with free wine and lots of students...

Several others had read their stories. She was thinking of going for a martini with them, yet had an early interview for her magazine the next day, and anyway, felt almost too happy to socialize. Trying to work out the logic of her thoughts – was there any? – she noticed again a teenage boy at the back of the shop, leafing through books but glancing at her from time to time. He seemed... familiar... anxious, but... on the brink of saying something extraordinary to her...

She moved towards him.

'Mikey?' He nodded, too choked up to speak. Tears rushed to Emma's eyes. Her brother, Mikey. They hugged, both gulping back tears, trying not to attract attention – though that was impossible. Other customers must have thought they were lovers, reunited after a long time. That maybe the young man had been in the military. They moved apart, looked at each other, laughing and crying at the same time.

The last time she'd seen him had been in care – one foster parent, cranky and old, had fostered them both for a while. Then sent him back as she "couldn't manage" them both; she said Mikey was "butter wouldn't melt", but then she caught him tearing up one of her photographs of her late husband. To her neighbors, he was "the sweetest boy on earth", always smiling and laughing – but then when he thought he wasn't being overheard, he broke things and said rude words. He wouldn't eat the stuff she cooked – smiling, saying he wasn't hungry – and then took cookies from her cupboard. After that they were fostered separately, until they were adopted. Cathy – they didn't know where she was sent.

Mikey hugged her as though she was his mom. Which she had been when he was little. As the eldest of the three children, she had to look after them as best she could when they were left alone all day and night.

She'd throw lit matches onto the wood in the grate in an attempt to ignite it. She'd use a broom handle to reach up to open the door bolt to go out into their tiny rubbish-filled yard. She'd wrap the kids in blankets and old coats to warm them up; tell them stories to cheer them up. If they heard a police siren outside, they'd all hide – Mom had been involved with the cops more than once. Mostly they fell asleep watching TV, which they kept on all the time.

When Mom came back, she was often ill and went to bed. A couple of neighbors had seen them all, seen how thin they were, their dirty clothes, and sometimes left groceries – cookies, fruit, juices – outside the door. It was they who tipped off welfare about the neglect.

Mikey told Emma he was working as a bottle-washer during the day, and bartending at night. That was the bit he enjoyed, though it paid only tips. He could play the guitar. He shared a room with three other boys in the Bronx. He never contacted his adoptive parents.

'When I was put with them, I pretended – I acted the way they wanted me to act. Always smiling and putting on a show. I only cried when I was in bed.'

'I did the same,' said Emma. 'I never felt they were Mom and Dad. They always wanted something from me. I felt like something they'd chosen in a store.'

'You were my mom, Emma. I missed you so much when we were split up.'

He'd seen her name and a blurred picture on a flyer left at the restaurant he worked in.

'I wasn't sure it would be you. I had this feeling.'

'Come back to my place, Mikey – don't go back to that awful room tonight. Have you had anything to eat? Do you like spaghetti Bolognese?'

They ate in her beautiful room. Sometimes talking, sometimes sitting and holding hands. Sometimes with tears in their eyes.

'Isn't it wonderful we're both in New York? And we found each other – you found me.'

'Yes. But I won't be here so long,' he said sadly. 'There's a better job up for grabs in L.A. It's a branch of the same club I work at now. They've said I have landed it... it's kind of moving up in entertainment. I might even get a few guitar gigs at this place. You could come and see me, couldn't you? I know it's a long way.'

'I don't really fly,' she admitted. 'But I could maybe take the train.'

It was late – Mikey had to be at work for ten-thirty the next day.

'You could stay here tonight! You could get the bus downtown from here... you'll be so much more comfortable than at the horrid place you're in. I've got a spare toothbrush and stuff. Hot water! We could have breakfast together – I've got Danish and coffee, juice.'

'I will stay – I don't want to leave now. It's like... home.'

They cuddled up in Emma's large bed – just like when he was little.

'It's so warm here – it's cold where I am. The heating doesn't always work. But I've found you now.'

Soon he was asleep, while Emma, fired with wonder, couldn't drop off. Dear, sweet Mikey – her baby, her little boy... he'd survived.

The morning was a rush. It was lovely to wake up with him, to have coffee and pastries together, to see he was eating.

'Emma... could I come back tonight? I'll pick up a few things from my place and do my bar shift, so it might be late… I don't want to leave now… can you put up with me? I'll be leaving for the new job in three weeks.'

She'd already planned to ask him if he'd liked to stay.

'It's your home too – we're family. Proper family.'

Every day she marveled that Mikey was with her, looked forward to cooking for him, chatting with him, listening to stories of how he grew up, his plans for a career in entertainment.

'My adoptive parents already had their own girl,' he told her. 'She was nice to me at first, but after a while she was always putting me down. And they were always on her side. I don't know why they even wanted another kid. It was like I was a huge problem. I left soon as I could. It wasn't hard to get a job in New York – places always want washers-up and kitchen help. I share with two of the guys from the place I work, and another guy – he waits tables somewhere else. We're always tired. You have to work fast. The chefs are always in a bad temper. But you get food at work – we all eat at work, mostly. Burgers and chicken and fries, we can have any soft drink we choose.'

The joy of having enough food to eat – and things to choose from. She and Mikey would never forget being so hungry that they cried with misery.

Each night they snuggled up together, his head cradled in her shoulder, like when he was small. Never had she felt so warm, so content. In the night she'd wake and stroke his face; sleepily, he'd respond.

'I love you, Emma,' he whispered. 'I'll never forget the way you looked after us... I wouldn't be here if it wasn't for you.'

They were locked in a close embrace. As close as you could get. Was it too close? Emma didn't care. He was her little brother. Nothing would happen.

The next morning was the day he was leaving. She took a photograph of him. How good-looking he was! Together, she knew they looked a fine couple.

Brother and sister. For always.

They promised to keep in touch.

But she never heard from him again.

Her sleep became worse. She enjoyed being a guest editor – lots of events, interviews, free gifts of cosmetics and clothes – and the editor said she was confident she'd have a fulltime job for Emma in about eighteen months.

Taking half a pill to sleep definitely helped, but she felt drowsy the next day. What worked better was meeting Jonathan two weeks after Mikey left – at a poetry reading, where he sat, one eyebrow raised, slouching back in his seat as though the whole thing was a joke. Which it was, in a way – but Emma liked the atmosphere and the free wine and the feeling of being alive, really alive.

Clutching her glass of Sauvignon, she wandered round the smoky, candlelit basement after the reading. There were prints on the wall – not particularly good, but worth a look. Gazing at them, she knew he was at her shoulder.

'Don't tell me you go in for all this stuff?' he started.

'What "stuff"'?' she said, coolly.

'This poetry crap. These amateur daubs. Those pseuds. This…'

'If you find it all so… distressing… why are you here?'

'On the off chance I'd meet someone like you. And now I have.'

That was The Beginning. He was an award-winning intern at New York Hospital, destined for a high-flying career as a doctor. He was seven years older than she. He'd done some military service as a para med. His family was wealthy – old Long Island money. His parents wanted him to settle down… like they'd settled down. Their shared love of irony and frivolity, combined with an unhealthy desire to work too hard, and a certain interest in sex (both were too intelligent not to know *that* would burn out before too long, become comfortable but routine, and then perhaps occasional and more exciting, before having to be excavated now and then) – it all worked. The chemistry worked.

She was slightly frightened of him… and that was part of the thrill. She knew that once she stopped being afraid of him, most of the thrill would be gone. She also knew, inevitably, familiarity would stop that heart-thumping fear. No one could hold on to it for long. It had to be replaced with… beauty, comfort, a life that would cushion. When that erotic fear had vanished, the beautiful life would remain.

*

Planning décor for a glamorous Manhattan apartment, with sound-proofed windows and walls, a gorgeous view from the sixteenth floor, real Picasso paintings, antique Turkish rugs, Emma was in heaven. She imagined it all, collected a folder of furnishing ideas.

'I don't want to give up my job – it starts in eighteen months, it's a plum job, and I have my own writing as well,' she reminded Jonathan.

'Of course, Em. I'm on track for some serious promotion – it'll mean working fourteen-hour days at least, and there are two research papers I want to publish. In medicine, what you've published makes you. The more you do, the more you're offered.'

Life was perfect: being in love was the best anti-depressant you could have.

To fill in before the job at *Mademoiselle*, she had a not-unpleasant job in a city bookstore. Her happiness carried her through every transaction... her smiling face attracted customers, her gentle, sound advice increased sales. She had new books to read, there was a good coffee shop next door, and she could be her impeccably groomed self, in black linen capris and silk shirts, chic flats, plain gold jewelry, perfect manicures.

'You always look so neat, Emma!' the manager told her. 'It's as though you've stepped from a fashion magazine.'

She often met Jonathan after work for a quick cocktail or a sandwich in a bar; they hadn't moved in together yet. At one point soon, they would. Within three weeks, they acknowledged they were in love, and would marry.

It won't last, she thought. This won't last.

It didn't.

When she began to be sick in the mornings, they were both appalled.

'Emma, for Christ's sake, you always use that thing!'

'I don't like... inserting it. Sometimes I get it wrong. It hurts. Oh God, what will we do?'

Jonathan took charge.

'Emma, this can be dealt with and it needn't alter our lives. All that's important is that you stay well and don't dwell on it. Emma, look at me... all will be fine.'

Fine? She couldn't have an abortion – they were illegal. And if it was in any way linked with Jonathan, his career – his brilliant career – would be over. But she couldn't have the baby either. It could be... it might be... she didn't want to think about it. Telling Jonathan was unthinkable. What had she done? How could it be wrong?

'Jonathan, this is terrible. I can't bear it.'

'It's not as terrible as you think, and you will be able to bear it. You'll be amazed, once this is over, how quickly you can forget. Start again. It's happened to so many women – girlfriends of doctors I know. And in a year or two, it's as though it never happened. That's if you can... be strong. I'll help you. It's just a few months, and then everything will be the same as before. It's not a terminal illness. And anyone can get through a few months... Emma, you'll be OK. You'll put it behind you. We'll be OK. You'll see.'

But she knew he'd been accepted, as an outstanding student, for a junior medical fellowship in London, for one year. They'd planned to marry when he returned. She'd be starting her own job on the magazine then. Miserable, sick, frightened, Emma went to California. She wrote to her close friends, Ruth and Mia, that she was in California for a while "to work out a temporary problem". She knew they'd understand – her situation wasn't unknown at Vassar. Jonathan had relatives in California, with a house on the ocean, where she could stay – he'd make all the arrangements. Everything. She didn't need to worry about a thing. She could live with an ocean view and work on her stories – until the time came. And then – what? Maybe she'd have a miscarriage. That was on the back of her mind. A stillbirth... why not? Above all, she didn't want to see... the child.

The next few months were a blur... she concentrated on her writing, made it clear to medics that she didn't want this baby.

'I want it removed.' And if there was anything they could do...?

MARRIAGE

When it's born, she's put under, and later she keeps her face turned to the wall when they bring the baby to her.

'Don't you want to see this sweet little thing?' one nurse asks.

She's furious. Didn't Jonathan say he'd informed the staff not to try to interest her in the baby? Didn't he promise that? In fact, they say the baby is weak – breathing problems – but she doesn't want to talk about it. Doesn't want to see the baby. It has nothing to do with her.

Jonathan calls her.

'It's all over now,' she says. She doesn't feel too bad – remnants of the "happy gas" they must have given her?

'I'll see you before I leave for London, Emma – in fact I'll pick you up from California next week. I'll fly down. We'll take the train back. We'll have three days together. Tell me you're feeling better already?'

'I am,' she says. 'It's such a relief. I feel free again. You were right.'

'I'm always right. I'm a doctor!' He laughs. 'The main thing is that you're OK?'

They keep reassuring each other they're both alright before Emma lies back and luxuriates in no longer being pregnant. Jonathan has sent her some flowers for her room, and books he knew she wanted. The joy of being able to start over! Her magazine job to look forward to in a few months... she could complete more stories...

She dropped off to vivid dreams of being on a train and losing all her luggage, running from carriage to carriage searching for it, finding it with all the contents thrown over the floor, trying to find something there, something vital, something important... small, mewing.

What?

They'd booked the date for their wedding. She'd chosen a dress – something simple. Unlike other brides, she wasn't obsessed with the details, had always thought wedding obsession trite. She put a box of novels on her wedding list – Barnes & Noble would package them for you in a wooden hamper. Jonathan's parents said they'd buy the books and asked her to choose thirty titles she wanted. Emma was in heaven – who cared about sheets and toasters when you could have crisp, new novels, evenings of pleasure?

At the same time, they did receive some gorgeous linen, crockery, silver cutlery, antique jugs for flowers and old, flowery serving dishes. Emma wanted all white for most things, but asked for "old and faded" for dishes. Jugs, serving plates, casseroles. Embroidered tablecloths and napkins. Guest towels, tea towels. Most of the guests understood "old and faded" – especially Emma's friends – but Jonathan's doctor friends were baffled.

'How about a juicer or a coffee-maker?' asked one. 'My wife thinks old china isn't hygienic.'

'Sure, anything,' was Jonathan's reply, when Emma wasn't in earshot.

Marriage and her work – the two things she loved. Or – shouldn't that be – Jonathan and her work? She certainly loved the comfort they lived in, their maid service – Carla was marvelous. She'd told Jonathan little about her early years – mainly because she avoided thinking about them – but she was never abused as a child. She was neglected, left so hungry that when taken into care, she was suffering from malnutrition. Emma was prepared for adoption. She stayed with a number of foster parents, mostly elderly and strict. One family even checked on the food she ate, writing on her report, *Emma may have stolen from our food cupboard.*

When she was adopted – to a pleasant middle-aged childless couple – she telephoned her best friend at her previous school.

'There's always plenty of food here! I can have cookies whenever I want, we have meatloaf. I choose what sandwiches I want to take to school – they never forget my bag lunch. Usually I have tuna or chicken, with potato chips and a banana. Milk! For breakfast, eggs and ham, or waffles and syrup, whatever I like! I'm never hungry anymore.'

'That's what parents are for.' Her friend's cool response.

Kids at her new school noted her fine clothes, her delicious lunches – she was sometimes known as

Emma-who-gets-everything-she-wants. She made one or two close friends as well – one who'd been temporarily fostered, and understood Emma's background. Friends to whom she could admit she was once sent to school without any underwear on – and had to tell the teacher, "Mommy forgot".

She lost touch with her brother and sister then – all three were considered so needy that they had to have separate families, and these were at different ends of the state. At eighteen, they could all leave home – she had no idea where they lived now, and felt if she ever did meet them again – such a sweet but painful memory, so painful – she'd never stop crying.

Yes, marriage suited her.

Being married and working, living in their apartment – that first year was wonderful. And also tiring – she had to keep a lot of lists in her head: what they needed, what they were running out of. Had she put the laundry out, remembered to send thank-you cards, booked repair men for their various essential machines, left the maid a shopping list and cash? Did she have the tickets for her dry-cleaning? Would she have time to shop for new shoes in her lunch hour? Her work at *Mademoiselle* was demanding: she loved it, dealing with fiction.

One day around lunchtime, she was called to the editor's office and fired. She'd been at the magazine three years.

'It's not you, Emma,' said Veronica, the editor. 'The company is in trouble and we're forced to make cuts. I have no choice – and of course I'll give you a good reference. Having worked here won't do your résumé any harm. But the job you do can be incorporated into the role of one of the senior writers. New technology is coming in, and while it has its good points, it does mean we need fewer staffers. We'll be able to give you a pay-off – not a lot, but some – and we may be able to use you as a freelance, but that's up to the department heads. They're all having to slice their budgets.'

She cleared her desk while colleagues tried not to notice, or murmured sympathetic phrases. *They're just glad it's not them*, she thought savagely – though one day it would be.

At home, she poured a large glass of Chablis and lay on the sofa. She was still too shocked to cry, but when Jonathan arrived, she sobbed.

'Emma, you'll get something else,' said Jonathan, gently. 'This is happening everywhere – even hospitals are reducing admin staff because machines can do certain basic technical tasks now.'

'I don't care!' she screamed, then regretted it. 'I'm sorry – of course I do care – but I've given so much to the magazine, worked through the night, given up weekends...' Jonathan let her cry, stroking her hair.

'I'm certain you'll get something else, with that excellent reference, and your dazzling résumé. Try to relax, Emma, let the first shock pass, be as angry as you like. I promise you'll be more relaxed tomorrow. And will get something else just as good.'

*

In this he was wrong. At first it was not unpleasant – not to have to bound out of bed and get dressed, made-up and groomed in thirty minutes. But it was only relaxing for a few minutes, as she lay there staring around her room. Jonathan was always up well before six – he liked to be first in at his department. She spread all her papers – copies of her résumé, copies of her reference – on her desk and worked through the few job ads. They wanted more than a writer. The most frequent magazine ad was for "production editor". That job now included writing, proofing, commissioning, as well as seeing the whole process through from page plan to print. One person doing the job of four.

'I could go to classes,' she told herself. 'But I don't want to. The only thing I can do is write.' She sent out applications on spec, but the reply was always the same. "Thanks, but no thanks. Good luck."

She was desperate for the job she'd lost. The comfort of the apartment didn't console her. Preparing dinner for Jonathan lost its charm when she had all day to think about it. The afternoons were the worst. In the morning, she had energy to send out applications, and research vacancies. In the evening, there was their meal together, a glass of wine and Jonathan to talk to. In the afternoon, she'd sometimes cry or go to bed, putting on her alarm ready to make dinner.

'Emma, what about the stories you used to write? When you were at Vassar?' Jonathan asked gently one evening. 'I haven't heard you talk about them lately.'

'Because, Jonathan, I've been trying to get a new job!' she snapped. 'You have to be in the right frame of mind to write fiction. I can't do it while I'm worried about being unemployed. I loved that job.'

'I know you did. But why not give job-hunting a rest for a bit? Make a timetable and write fiction for part of the day, then go out and enjoy yourself a bit. You could meet me at the hospital – some days – and we could have a quick snack in the canteen. It's not cordon bleu, but not too bad. I'm worried about you, Emma.'

She thought. She'd had two stories published in the magazine, and two more in literary journals. In four years. Was she energized enough to try again?

The next day she bought a new notebook and, in a coffee shop, ordered an espresso and began to jot down ideas. One was a story about a woman like her, who'd lost her publishing job because of "cuts" and created a new one – as a high-class escort. No one "needs" magazines – but people always need sex, was her premise. She created a classy, clever heroine working from her own apartment, charging lots of money on a rising scale of service – from conversation to bondage. Many of the men just wanted conversation. Emma had always known how vulnerable and lonely men were, always wanting to be reassured, mothered.

The story gathered pace without any graphic descriptions at all and was accepted by the first magazine she sent it to, an intelligent glossy for women. The editor then asked if she had a second story in the pipeline – and her new career began.

She concentrated on "literary" short stories with a touch of noir, aimed at women like her: graduates, bright, maybe single, or married with one or two children, living in comfort on a good income, yet still prone to the slings and arrows of their emotional lives. Disappointed with marriage. Sometimes she set a story in France, but mostly they were Manhattan stories. She was candid with her thoughts: she'd open her soul to the page. And she was on the side of women: her male characters came over as vain, sexually selfish, frail, lazy, generous, protective, patronizing, needy, difficult. Her women: clever, disillusioned, emotionally fragile, housework-haters, perceptive, escapees from their jealous mothers, adored by their fathers, endlessly criticized by their small children.

She'd seen how her friends – brilliant, glorious Vassar alumni – ran around their little children, having to respond to questions like, "When do we get our supper, Mom? You haven't even laid that table yet, have you!" or "You're not wearing that tonight, are you? You can see everything! It's rude!" Or their husbands: "Any chance of a clean shirt round here?" or "What have you done to your hair? I liked it the way it was." These glorious beauties, chosen by their professors as "The Girl to Sleep With" because of their looks and their brains, now facing daily court martials on why they bought "the wrong" cereal, forgot to wash gym kit, failed to pick up a business suit from the dry cleaner.

As she sold more stories, her morale lifted higher and higher. Yes, it was lonely – writing always was that – but she didn't *feel* lonely. This was a wonderful time for her, after losing her job. Then Eve her agent rang to say a TV company was interested in making a series from her "clever call girl" stories, as they described them. A TV series!

'They want at least five story lines for a series,' Eve told her. 'I thought – a different male taste for each episode? It's a late-night thing – you can be fairly black. It occurred to me your character could have a different style of hair and clothes for each episode – to add more visual interest. What do you think? An hour each time.'

It really wasn't hard to write each episode. What was hard was working with the TV script people – far more nitpicking and critical than any print journalist she'd ever worked with. After each script conference, she came home exhausted.

'I thought it would be exhilarating,' she complained to Jonathan over dinner. 'Instead I feel they're always picking my stuff to pieces. It's almost as though I wasn't the author. So much fuss over sets, entrances, lighting, props, dialogue cut to the bone, whole bits changed...'

'You'll feel so much better when the series is shown. It's "all you've ever dreamed of".'

The women's magazine cliché was supposed to make her laugh, but she only said, 'Yes, I suppose so.'

'You "suppose so"? For Christ's sake, Emma, most writers would be in heaven! Think how you were feeling when you lost your job. Did you imagine this sort of success? And it's all down to you, your talent. For God's sake, enjoy it.'

She saw what he meant and felt guilty, ashamed – that old familiar feeling. While the first episode was being made, she rewrote the script four times – then they brought in another scriptwriter to "help" her.

'I know you might get jaded, writing over and over again,' the producer said. 'You're doing a wonderful job! This is going to be huge! Huge!'

The new scriptwriter was polite but not over-friendly.

'Just a few tweaks,' he said. 'You've probably got too close to your work. That's happened to me in the past. Take a break for a few days – I'll call you if I need any info.'

He didn't call. When she went a week later for a script meeting, she barely recognized her work.

'The heroine is meant to be bright, possibly a Vassar girl, with a clear understanding of men's psychology. She isn't a caricature,' she said, glacially. It was the first time she'd been so outspoken. There was a silence, a shifting of papers.

'Well... coffee, everyone? A short break, I think.'

She was crying when Jonathan came home.

'They'll pay me what we agreed, but use only their own scriptwriter. My name will just be as creator of the story – but I didn't write that garbage they'll be using!'

'Did you speak to Eve?'

'Of course. She recommended compromise, putting up with their changes, basically not making a fuss, not getting a reputation for being "difficult". It's important to be easy to work with.' She spat out the last words. 'On the magazine I was known for being the ideal person to work with! I was never "difficult"! If I'd had my own material, I'd have been delighted. So why should some new graduate be the boss of my work? I can't stand him. But if this stuff goes out, it'll make me look like a jerk.'

Jonathan doubted that.

When Eve told her the series had been pulled – though she'd still get the money – she was shocked.

'It's not the differences in script approach – more that they have new guidelines now. Or they say they do. They feel the nature of the story line, though original, might be too much for their audience. They've shelved it – but that doesn't mean you can't rework it in some way and submit elsewhere. TV companies do this all the time. It's what they do. Emma? Are you OK?'

MANHATTAN, 1972

'Em, I have new colleagues I'd like to ask for drinks – not a party, just drinks,' he said, looking round her office, piled high with towers of paper and folders and books. He had a highball in his hands, but she knew the kitchen was not well provisioned. 'Do you think – with the help of Carla, maybe other maids? – we could get the apartment looking decent?'

She could no longer snap back that it already looked "decent". It wasn't fair on Jonathan, was it? Cleaners were much harder to come by. She hadn't been feeling well.

'I'll try, when is it you'd like to invite them?'

'A week next Friday,' he said, firmly.

She took a pill the next day to pep her up. She sat, phone and directory in hand. Three cleaners could come, charging a huge cash sum for four hours, though they'd only stay one – the logic was explained, but she gave up trying to understand. A surly window cleaner took her address, queried it, then snapped, 'I've worked in the city fourteen years but can't be expected to know every back alley!'

This isn't a back alley – far from it, she was tempted to snarl, but instead sweetly gave him instructions.

She needed a laundress – ironing was piling up. 'We'll have to charge you double for such short notice – take it or leave it,' the laundry said. She took it. She explained to Carla that they needed extra help, it would be too much for her – but Carla wasn't keen on this. Wearily, Emma had to tactfully explain again – the preparations hadn't even started yet and already she felt stressed.

By phone, she charged a case of wines and champagne, a tray of canapes, a dish of fruit, for the look of it, and a bucket of flowers. Then she went back to bed. That's all.

The next day she was up at seven waiting for the window cleaner who'd promised to arrive at eight. By ten no one had turned up – the cleaners were also supposed to be there at eight, the laundress nine. Migraine flickers started. She took a headache pill, half a tranquilizer... and still had a dull version of the headache left.

At ten past ten they'd all arrived, but since everyone wanted coffee, they didn't begin. The maids chatted to each other, the laundress picked out the ironing as though it was dirty, not clean, the window washer slammed down windows and wrenched them up as loudly as he could and slopped buckets of water about.

The laundress grumbled, 'I won't be able to finish this lot, Mrs. Bowden. There's enough for another day here. You should have told the agency how much there was to get through.'

If you'd turned up on time it would have been fine. 'Do I have to pay for the missed hour?'

'What missed hour? We're allowed a half hour for our lunch but I didn't eat the bag lunch I brought with me. I went on working and made it up then.'

It was an hour, not half, thought Emma, but by now fizzing sparks were running through her head.

'You also have to pay my cab fare – it's in the contract.'

Wordlessly she handed the money over, and the laundress barged out the door. She'd already paid the window washer – who'd done a good job – but the maids said they "had another appointment", and didn't wash the bathroom or kitchen floors. Carla did.

On the day of the drinks, the apartment was shining, windows gleaming, floors waxed, flowers arranged, drinks chilling, canapes and vodka jellies cooling. The view of Manhattan through the gleaming windows was stunning – that was when Emma felt her best. It did help, seeing how beautiful the apartment looked.

Emma knew she looked perfect – a red linen dress with a halter neck, her blond hair newly highlighted, some old silver drop earrings. But it was one of her bad days. She'd got up early planning to go to the club, had coffee, then – looking in the mirror and seeing how awful she looked first thing – gone back to bed. The warmth, the comfort, the relief of snuggling down again. She calculated she could sleep all morning. First, she'd have another coffee, with cream this time... and a biscuit topped with thick chocolate... then sleep. She took off her dress. Lay down. Soon it would be drinks time.

Emma? Emma? Is that you? It's you, isn't it? I'm coming to find you, Emma. To find you... ha ha ha!

No. NO...

She got up again, heart thumping.

When the guests arrived, she knew instantly she'd hate the evening. Both wives were over-enthusiastic about the apartment, asking her where she'd bought the Persian rugs (she had no idea) and what was the story behind the Picasso. She had none – they'd bought it because they liked it.

'Didn't he paint a lot of clowns?' asked one wife.

No, that was someone working for Woolworth's, Emma thought, but said, 'Did he? I'm not sure I've seen those.'

The men, as usual, launched into complaints about their department and some "questionable" research (questionable and fallible were their two favorite words).

'How's your novel going? What's it about?' the other wife asked. Emma hated not being asked about her work, and she hated even more being asked about it.

'Quite well. I'm superstitious about talking about work in progress.'

'Oh. Well, we'll look forward to seeing it in Barnes and Noble.'

Without warning, the drowning of the little girl at the party came up. There'd been a similar tragedy last week, at the home of a film director.

'Do you recall that – at Carter's apartment?' said one wife. 'Shocking. We were there, actually – five years ago? Six? So terrible for the parents...'

'Weren't they holding on to her hand?' said the other wife.

'I imagine so... but kids escape quickly. They were devoted to her, they always brought her with them to parties,' the first wife said.

'Obviously they loved parties, but don't parents sometimes have to make choices?'

'Maybe this one wasn't suitable for such a small girl. Clearly it wasn't,' said Emma.

'It was a tragic accident, Emma,' said Jonathan.

'I imagine the little girl wandered on to the terrace then fell in – the sunlight gets very bright there. She may have been dazzled,' said one of the husbands.

'But wasn't it a totally avoidable, unnecessary death?' She didn't admit she and Jonathan had been there. They had been there, hadn't they? She remembered the good-looking Italian cop peering at the Picasso...

'Many accidental deaths are – in fact, most,' said Jonathan; then, eager to elevate the mood, asked, 'Top-ups, everyone? Champagne? And do have more of Em's lobster canapes.'

'You made these yourself?' cried one of the wives. Emma pretended she had, and led them away from the melancholy byway. The dinner widened into a cheerful, pointless evening of "bonding". The wives swapped recipes, favorite TV programs, favorite male actors, and stores where you could buy vegetables that tasted of something. Flower arranging classes. And anecdotes about their children. Their witty, wonderful, clever children.

Thinking about the child toppling into the pool, she thought she had been close by when it happened... but had she? Or was she aware of the blur of figures, the chaos? She remembered they left soon after the paramedics arrived – Jonathan instantly asking if he could help, but the child was already dead by then. The paramedics shook their heads. The parents left with the ambulance and the child... the party was over. Men downed brandies; women cried. She remembered them going home in a state of shock, yet because of the adrenalin she had a sense of lightness, of well-being. Hadn't she sat and talked – really talked – with Jonathan that night?

'Great news, Emma!' said Eve, ringing her in the morning. 'Wonderful news. Warner Brothers have taken an option on *Diary* – they think it would make a good film. With Diane Keaton. They're offering a good fee. What do you think?'

'Think? I'm thrilled. This is so... surprising. I had no idea...'

'They see it as a feminist kind of film – though I know you didn't intend that. And they'll use their own scriptwriter. This time, will you agree to that? Remember, it's still an option. It's when they start shooting that we can really celebrate – but I have a positive feeling about this.'

'Yes!' she gasped. To be given a second chance... like a dream. The times she'd slumped, miserably wishing she'd handled the TV series better all those years ago. Longing to be given a second chance.

Wishing she could rewind everything. And it was her birthday. Forty... six.

She wandered happily round the apartment. She called Jonathan. 'It's only what you deserve,' he said. 'And on your birthday! We'll celebrate tonight.'

'It's still only an option,' she parroted. 'It's when they start shooting you can really celebrate.'

They did start casting – with Diane Keaton and Ryan O'Neal in leading roles. Emma hoped she'd be asked to look at the script – give her opinion – but she wasn't.

'That wasn't part of the deal, Emma,' Eve reminded her. 'Remember you said how much you'd give for this? And didn't want to make the error you did with that other series? These people are all the same. They like to do it their way. It'll take eighteen months or two years to make.'

No one ever asked Emma for her advice, though Eve seemed to be in touch with Warner Brothers.

'It's coming along well,' she said. Was all she said. 'Now's the time to work on your next project – when things are so successful, it's the best time. Don't let things slide. This is a good time for you, Emma.'

It was and it wasn't. While thrilled – longing to see the film – she had problems getting started on a new novel. She'd made false starts, made notes, got down ideas – but nothing really gelled.

'I can't seem to manage it... it's just too hard,' she complained to Jonathan. Where had she heard these words before? When she was a child... her real mother? Foster parents? They all said it.

*

Three years after their visit to Cathy, she had a phone call. Tearful, incoherent. Noises of people chatting in the background, someone asking for a bag of sugar, laughter.

'Emma? It's me, Cathy.'

'How are you?'

'Not so good.' Sobs. 'Do you think I could possibly stay with you for a little while? Would that be trouble for you?' She sobbed again. 'I can't think of any place else to go.'

Emma's heart sank, but she felt sad about her sister. 'I'm sure you can, Cathy. Is there... what's wrong?'

'Wayne's been sick. It's changed him. We've had a lot of fights. His mother's here and she wants to take the kids while he gets better. Emma, he gets so angry and rough – I can't stand it. The kids would be OK with her. The trailer's a mess, she bawled me out for it, but I don't have the energy, sometimes I walk the kids to school and then get back into bed, at least it's warm there. Wayne's mostly asleep, but has to get up when the medics come, they come every day with injections, he's not supposed to drink, but when they've gone, he starts, and I have to buy it. There's no money left for food. I have to get away. I can't stand it.'

She was sobbing harder now.

'Cathy, you can stay with us,' Emma said, knowing already what problems would lie ahead, how Jonathan would react, how her own sympathy would run out. How her precious privacy, her lovely home – and her sleep – would be invaded. 'How will you get here? I'll pay for your flight.'

'I've never done that. Where would I get the ticket? I don't know how to do it. Could you... could you get me a ticket and post it? The kids are leaving with his ma tomorrow. Wayne wants me to get out quickly.'

'Yes, I'll do that and I'll put in some bills to get you to the airport – get a cab. You have to phone them first and tell them where to pick you up. Is it a store you're calling from? They'll have cab numbers there. Once you're at the airport, ask one of the airport staff to show you where to go. It's cold here – bring some warm things. It'll be OK.'

'Write me with the details. Write soon, Emma! I'll come soon as I can – will they book flights that quick? I've never been in a plane. Is it very frightening? They say it is. But I've got to do it...'

'I'll send you a couple of sedatives. Take one before you board – get on the plane, I mean. Then another if the journey gets rocky – but I'm sure it won't.'

'Thanks.' Cathy sobbed. 'I knew you'd say yes.'

Predictably, Jonathan was not sympathetic. A few "Christs", two trips to their bar for large Scotches, questions of "How long for?" and "What will we do with her?"

Questions she couldn't answer.

'She's my sister. She sounded in despair, I couldn't say no.'

'Wouldn't a hotel be better? She'd still be near you – I'll take care of the bills – maybe one with a pool and spa? Give her a luxury break?'

'Jonathan, she wouldn't be happy in a hotel,' she

said. 'She'd feel uncomfortable. Guests and staff would look down on her.'

She knew what he was thinking.

'I'll be the one who's uncomfortable if she's here, for Christ's sake!'

'It'll be fine – I imagine she'll want to sleep a lot and talk a lot, but you don't have to be involved. We can have dinner, then you've got your study to work in. Your meetings. I'll go for walks with her, show her round. Maybe a movie. I don't know. I wish I did. I'm sorry.'

'Fine,' he groaned. Then knocked back a third Scotch.

When the large, lumpy figure, dressed in a shabby gray coat, weighted down by a military rucksack, came shakily, anxiously into Arrivals, Emma ran forward to embrace her.

'Cathy! How was your flight? Did you need those pills?'

'I took one, but I've still got that second one. It was OK – the food was nice, we had chicken and potatoes, and a trifle in a little paper cup – it's so big here! And noisy! Why are all those people holding signs up with names on? Hi, Jonathan.'

'Cathy,' he said, and embraced her lightly.

'Where's your luggage?'

'In my rucksack. I didn't bring much. Mainly pictures of the kids and some toys to remind me of them.'

'But you'll be seeing them before long,' Emma reminded her.

Cathy said nothing.

*

Emma had made their guest room as welcoming as she could. A Victorian jug covered with pansies and filled with pink roses and blue hydrangeas. Terracotta sheets under a patchwork comforter, faded pinks and blues, white walls. A thrift shop chest of drawers – one of Emma's finds that she'd painted in palest blue. Sanded floor boards, a pale pink and blue Turkish rug. Rose geranium soap, matching towels, flowers in the en suite bathroom too.

Cathy stared.

'All mine, Emma?' she said softly.

'All yours, Cathy. Now, unpack and we'll fix something to eat. Have a shower if you like – there's a hairdryer. The water's always hot.'

She left Cathy still staring round the perfect room.

Jonathan had already had his first drink.

'Can I get you something, Em? Wine? A martini?'

'Maybe a glass of Chablis. Carla's left us a roast chicken cooling. Then there's an ice cream trifle with chocolate sauce. She always liked ice cream.'

'Em, don't be nervous. I sense she's a little bit... high? The flight. What pills did you give her?'

'Just Equanil, Jonathan! I think you've had one or two yourself on a bad flight.'

'I may have,' he sighed. 'Best not to give her any more.'

Cathy said the dinner was "flavorsome". She dropped things and spilled her glass of beer – she'd said she liked only beer. She talked with her mouth open while she was eating.

Jonathan fled to his study. Cathy had a shower, but her hair – dark blond like Emma's – was still lank and greasy.

If only she could lose weight and try to groom herself, she'd be pretty.

Cathy talked mainly of her kids, saying it was "best" and "the right thing" they go to Wayne's mother.

'They love her. She's always giving them candy and toys. She's a widow. She has a big old house that was left her by an uncle with no kids. She and he were close.'

Too close.

'And your trailer? Does it belong to you?'

'It's in Wayne's name, we both put some money in – my adopted parents gave me some. But it's falling apart now. It's too much for me to handle in this cold weather. Wayne's getting worse, you know.' She cried again.

'Sleep as late as you like, Cathy. You and I can walk through the park tomorrow, if you like. Do you want to call the kids?'

'She don't have a phone, but I have a store number I can call some days. Maybe tomorrow.'

The next day they crunched through fallen leaves, saw squirrels. Cathy couldn't get over how tall the buildings were, how many well-dressed people there were.

'All wearing their best clothes! It's like they're all going to a wedding.'

She was still wearing her shabby outfit from yesterday. Delicately, Emma said, 'You didn't have space to pack much, would you like a couple of T-shirts, some new pants, a scarf maybe?'

'I have my own clothes,' Cathy muttered. 'I might get a scarf and gloves.'

They had lunch at a burger joint where Emma knew Cathy would feel at home. As they walked back, they bumped into a girl Emma knew from Vassar, now a radio presenter.

'This is my sister, Cathy. She's staying with us.'

'That's nice. How long are you staying, Cathy?'

'Don't know,' mumbled Cathy.

'Well, have a pleasant visit. Toodle-oo!'

Cathy turned to Emma. 'What's that mean?'

'It's an English expression, I think. Some people use it, mainly journalists. Sort of ironic. Camp.'

Cathy looked baffled.

Cathy stayed in bed, getting up late – and later, sometimes not until late afternoon – on most days. She preferred breakfast to any other meal – bacon and eggs, which Emma never had, but willingly cooked for her sister.

Carla did Cathy's room, her stiff back silently expressing her disgust. She picked up trash, threw away flowers in soured water, pushed dirty clothes into the washer. Emma showed Cathy how to use all the machines, but when she tried, she couldn't figure out the controls.

'You got too many machines,' she cried. 'I can't keep it all in my head. Could I have a cup of instant coffee? I don't like that stuff you say is real. Got any cream? Cookies?'

She didn't seem to miss her children, though she phoned Wayne's mother a few times.

'They're fine – she loves having them and they got that big house and garden to play in – but Wayne's getting worse. There's talk they'll move him to a hospital soon. How are we going to pay for that?'

'Do you think he'll recover?' Emma asked.

Cathy shook her head and went on looking through a magazine, one she'd bought herself, a cheap woman's weekly.

'Emma, could you loan me the cash for this?' She showed her a picture of fake jewelry. She was still wearing her old gray pants, but had a new black long-sleeved T-shirt Emma had bought for her. She seemed to be losing weight.

Carla phoned in sick. Emma prepared dinner for the three of them. She and Jonathan talked about politics and some new Truffaut movie, while Cathy sat sullenly.

'Would you like to see a film, Cathy?' asked Emma. 'Anything you wanted to see?'

'I prefer TV.'

She watched TV every day, as soon as she got up. Emma never watched it, except for an occasional old movie – the constant drone of it drove her mad. Cathy liked game shows.

'Look at that, Emma! She won the freezer and the car!'

'Yes,' Emma snapped.

She was working on her new novel, but not getting very far. Cathy had the TV on so loud, she was always aware of the jabbering voice and music.

'Could you... turn it down a little?' Emma asked.

Resentfully, Cathy switched it off.

'You don't have to switch it off. I just said lower the sound.'

'Everything I do is wrong! I'd rather be back in the trailer again. It's like a prison here.'

Crying, she flung herself onto the sofa.

Emma felt exhausted.

'Is it time to go back and look after the kids now?' she asked. 'And Wayne, how is he now?'

'He's in hospital. His ma said he ain't got long to go. He took too much drugs.'

The next day, the call came – Wayne had died that morning. Cathy said she wouldn't go to the funeral, and was glad he was "at peace".

'I won't have to see him no more, and that suits me,' she said.

'What about the kids?' Emma asked. 'Don't you have to go back and look after them?'

'Nope. His ma wants them. She thinks I'm an unfit mother. She's lied about me to welfare – said I did drugs, too. I did once, but that's all. Anyways, it's best they live with her – I can still see them. She got welfare and some inheritance from her uncle. Can I switch the set on again?'

Emma saw – realized at last – Cathy wasn't entirely normal. Didn't seem to have normal feelings. What could she say? Do? Only Jonathan could advise her.

'Em, I noticed it when she arrived,' he said as they sat in his study, talking quietly while Cathy watched a game show. 'She just settled in and trashed the place without a thought. I never felt she really missed those children. She feels comfortable and responsibility-free in this apartment, doing fuck all. I also think her IQ is low. She believes you'll always bail her out.'

'But what can we do?' she said. 'I'm not sure how much more I can stand. The mess, the noise...'

'The only thing we can do is set her up in a small apartment or decent hostel here, and see if she can get a cleaning or service job – she needs something to do. I can't see her going back now. Put it to her that we'll look in on her, help in any way, but we have a lot of work on and need the apartment to ourselves. Something like that. OK, old girl?'

Next day, Emma took an Equanil to fortify herself for the talk with Cathy. Once she was up and planted in front of the TV, Emma turned it off.

'Cathy, we have to talk about the... the future – lovely as it would be, we can't keep you here for ever – you need your independence. You said yourself it was like a prison sometimes.'

'I never meant it!' said Cathy. 'I want to stay. Please, let me stay. I got nowhere else – I'm never going back.'

'You can stay another two weeks while we look for somewhere you could live – a good hostel or a bedsit – there are nice ones round here – and get you set up. But you're going to need an income. Have you ever worked? Didn't you say you were a waitress once?'

'I couldn't work in a smart place, with smart people. Don't want no work anyway.'

'There are lots of cleaning and housekeeping jobs...' Emma started, then remembered the chaos and dirty clothes piling up in Cathy's room. 'Or, you could go back to school – take basic courses in office work?'

'No!'

'Then I don't see how we can help you! Unless...'

The picture of Cathy's little one came up again in Emma's mind. How sweet he was. She'd been thinking about him... could they...?

'How old is Scotty?'

'Nearly five years now. He's the baby.'

Five? A baby! A real baby to love and care for, save from poverty and mess. The baby. Her baby. Her real baby. The baby she deserved. She'd been thinking about it so much.

'Cathy, I know this must seem a strange idea and we'll talk about it again. But... do you think Jonathan and I should have Scotty and bring him up? He's so little. In return, we'll find you an apartment, fit it out and let you have an allowance for yourself. You wouldn't need to work then. And we'd be here...'

Cathy said nothing for a while.

'I don't know whether Wayne's ma will let him go,' she said. 'And he'd miss his brothers and sisters. But I'd rather have an apartment to myself. I don't want to look after no more kids. It's too hard.'

Is everything in life too hard? Maybe it is. That's what I've found out.

Jonathan heard Emma out, splashed Scotch in his glass, threw down some sort of "headache" tablet, though he “never, if he could possibly avoid it” took any kind of pill. There was silence for a while.

‘I’ve seen you looking at his picture and I know you think he’d help your life,’ he began. ‘He will be sweet and loving. And noisy and difficult, since he’ll be taken from his family. And – let’s be honest – we don’t know how bright he is. I want you to think carefully about this, let’s look at the benefits to us. You know how logic isn’t one of your strongest points.’

‘We can get help! There are some marvelous kindergartens in this area. And we’d be giving him a lovely start in life… think what fun it’ll be having a little one around.’

‘Will it? You never used to think that.’

‘I’m older and wiser now!’ she snapped.

‘And if he needs… special help?’

‘He was such a cute baby.’

‘He’s– what is he, five, now? About that? Hardly a baby.’

‘Please, Jonathan…’

‘Do you remember that evening at Carter’s? The little girl drowned in the pool? You said you had more sympathy for the mother who tried to drown her than for the little girl. She had brain damage. Emma, you do remember?’

‘Yes… of course. But this is different – he’s not brain-damaged, and you help kids by talking to them a lot, teaching them things. I bet all they did in the trailer was eat and watch TV.’

They argued on. Emma was determined to win, and she sensed Jonathan was not as against the idea as he thought. There was something... different... in his attitude. Finally, she said, 'He's the baby I... Jonathan, I want to have him now.'

Emma was as busy and happy as she'd ever been. Wayne's mother had said Scotty could come to them – she was finding five kids hard to manage and the welfare people thought it would be a good idea. There were forms to fill in, and there had been a visit from a welfare person in New York. That Emma herself had been adopted impressed her. She never mentioned Emma's past... the accident. After all, Emma was never accused or implicated. That was all over, finished. Emma wondered if she even knew about it.

'Your apartment is beautiful!' she said. 'And you'll have help, right? Scotty will be able to keep in contact with his family if he wishes? His grandmother is trying her best, but finding it hard to cope with all of them. We're trying to find help for her. You're OK about staying in touch?'

Yes. Yes. Yes. To all of this, yes.

Excitement fueled her. She could hardly sleep.

They rented Cathy a small loft nearby. She'd found a new boyfriend, a bar bouncer. Emma didn't see her much.

Because Emma is family, the adoption process won't be difficult, the welfare woman reassures her. Jonathan and Emma go down twice to see Scotty, who's really too little to do anything but laugh at the gifts they bring, and clown around. Wayne's mother is by turns sullen and ingratiating; she sees clearly the benefits of Scotty living with them. Welfare say he should be with them for two months to settle in before they sign anything legal. A date to pick him up and take him to New York is agreed. They leave more gifts and their own photographs with him. Emma hugs him when she leaves. He responds, eyes sparkling.

Emma turns her spare room into a nursery – the joy of buying toddler things: little pajamas and tiny socks and matching scarves and mittens. Soft toys, glove puppets, an elephant that squeaks, a gorgeous teddy bear. She chooses soft sunshine yellow for the walls, white woodwork, bedlinen with cute lion cubs on. She hires extra help ready to start when Scotty arrives. She wants to spend as much time with him as she can, not to be bothered by chores, but also to have some time for working. It's going to be bliss, she tells herself. Having a child. There's nothing like it. Nothing.

Then the letter arrives.

It's badly written.

It's from Wayne's mother:

We heard you killed a girl when you was at school – welfare, they told us. You never even mentioned it. As if we'd let Scotty come to you. We have canceled the arrangements. Got help from welfare now and that's better than letting Scotty live with a killer.

Emma sat with the letter in her shaking hand.

She feels she's aged thirty years. Looking in a mirror, she sees wrinkles spreading across her face, lines around her mouth, her eyes beginning to sink and lids hooded. Bits of gray have emerged in her hair, which has started to recede. She's aware this isn't really happening… or is it? When Jonathan gets home, she shows him the letter. And weeps, and sobs.

Ice clinking in glasses.

'Can we… appeal to welfare?' she whispers.

'Em, that won't help. We offered to have him, welfare aren't removing him because of neglect or anything – the decision is for his own family to make. Welfare will say their "hands are tied". That's what they'll say.'

'Then… what?'

'We could try adopting a kid through the conventional route. That takes time. More meetings, more paperwork. More… questions.'

'They won't let me! I can't go through this again. I wanted Scotty. I loved him. He was mine.'

'Yes.'

'Could Cathy do anything?'

'Seems to me she's lost interest in the kids. I don't think she has a grasp of much. She doesn't know about the accident, either, does she?'

'I've never told her.'

'She'll feel the same as the grandmother – if she feels anything. Thinks anything.'

Emma takes three Nembutals, a slug of Scotch, slowly gets into bed.

She'll send all Scotty's things to the thrift shop.

Don't think. Don't think. Don't think.

Los Angeles, 1961

Flying down to California, Jonathan worked through some reports and made notes. He took a glass of champagne from the stewardess, who flashed him a dazzling smile and called him "Prof" – a well-trodden flirtation routine, he guessed. Well, nothing doing.

Why did every woman these days look like Marilyn… or try to? The hair, the whispering voice, the make-up behind the smile – the put-on adoration. Behind the public image, Marilyn was a nervous wreck, he'd heard. It seemed most women were as fragile as Emma, women surgeons excluded. Those women had real balls. Seeing them in their combat gear and rubber boots, preparing for a brain op, was almost carnal. When they pulled off their protective caps and eyewear, you'd be shocked by a fall of shining hair, a pretty face – and intelligent conversation, usually about medical research or procedure complaints about the people who ran hospitals. Perfect. His type of woman.

A tricky landing, but not bad enough for an Equanil – the oxygen masks would have to be coming down for that. Before a flight, he took a couple of pills from Emma's large pharmacy – "candy store" – of drugs. She never noticed. He rarely used them.

He'd been trying to think – or not to think – why he was in California. Curiosity, mainly. Let's be honest, he told himself. Curiosity is stronger than many emotions, most of which are fake – produced to order. The way people produce tears at funerals because they think they have to, or they're responding to some emotional music – then spend a prolonged happy hour at the reception, laughing, chatting, eating and drinking. The noise levels rising. New trays of canapes and desserts being paraded out as the first lot vanish rapidly. The glasses refilled.

But you can't fake curiosity. Not fundamental curiosity. He had to know. To see. He was an eminent doctor now – he'd been lately described as New York's "top medic" in *The Trib*. He was forty-one.

He believed a doctor should have not just clinical, but intellectual skills – be an academic as well as a practical professional. And he already knew he wanted to specialize in what people could do to protect themselves – to reduce "avoidable" deaths, live longer, live better. He believed most deaths, from road accidents to heart attacks, could be avoided by more careful living. And he was interested in how kids grew up to become "careful livers" – to avoid obvious hazards, yet lead a fulfilling life. He knew it sounded like hopeless idealism, yet he was gaining a following. His research on avoidable deaths in New York City was already attracting some attention. He wasn't afraid to be outspoken, to pose embarrassing questions on TV and radio. He led several committees, was on various boards, gave seminars at the leading medical schools in the USA and abroad.

He'd made a promise to himself that he would see the child, take an interest – driven by curiosity rather than sentiment. Most men who'd been in his position preferred to forget, to wipe out the experience. He could understand that. Ten years on, this was his first visit. The friend who'd set up the adoption – and the adoptive parents, second cousins of his – understood this day would come at some point, and now it had.

He'd asked to see the child in a neutral setting – maybe sitting in a café with his mother. A preliminary "viewing". His friend – a doctor in California – walked with him to the café, where they casually looked at the menu in the window.

'The one in the red jersey,' said his friend.

Something constricted Jonathan's throat, his eyes became moist. He gripped his briefcase. The child was chatting and laughing with his mother, then studying the menu. The café door was open and Jonathan heard him say, 'Chocolate or vanilla? No, I think I had vanilla last time. Do they do the sprinkles with chocolate?' Then, hamming it up, he actually said, 'Le chocolat or le vanilla? What's the French for "or"?'

'It's "ou",' his mother said, smiling. 'And I think it's "vanille". I could be wrong.'

'I wish I could take my kitten to school. Don't you think Hero is a good name? Some stupid kids said it wasn't a cat's name. I don't care. Who wants a dull old cat named Blackie or Sooty? Here's our ice cream!'

Then the industrial threshing of a coffee machine, and Jonathan could hear no more. Or bear no more.

But as unbearable as it was for Jonathan, he couldn't

take his eyes off the smiling kid. Was this laughing child really his? Was this kid really OK? These were the questions that had dragged him to California, questions that at one moment were the most important and piercing he'd ever struggled with, yet in the next, the dumbest, most pointless.

He couldn't hear what the boy was saying now; there was traffic noise, and men were pulling down a building on the other side of the street. He didn't have much time; he couldn't stand on the sidewalk staring into the café for much longer. His friend had left: he thought Jonathan would like to be alone. Somebody would notice him staring in; it would arouse suspicion. He'd give it another minute at the café window. Three thousand miles across the country, and three thousand back for just a glimpse of this kid.

His hair color was similar, but what could that mean? It changes with the years and in California, perhaps, the climate. Jonathan went through the list – eye color, the mold of the nose, the shape of a smile, tell-tale mannerisms. It was impossible, this hurried study through a café window in a Los Angeles suburb.

Had he been a fool, wasting time on this?

In a bar on the next block, he sat morosely in front of his second whiskey highball. What did it matter, now, if the child was his or some other man's? Emma could have been seeing someone just before she met him. He was building his career on all this stuff about people cutting risk and curbing chance to avoid ill-health and keep death at bay. It was paying off in Manhattan. But here in this gloomy L.A. dive – a fat, bored blond washing glasses behind the bar; a senior sitting at a table by the men's room, waiting to die – he thought about the kid and happenstance.

He recalled a line he'd come across when he was dating a girl who was crazy about that old Puritan poet, Milton. *Chance governs all*, he'd written. What we do and who we do it with is all down to chance. The kid could have been any man's way back then: his or someone else's. But now they were on different roads. His in Manhattan, the boy's in L.A. That's the way it would have to stay.

He had a few hours to kill before setting off for his return flight. He'd kill them in this bar.

MANHATTAN, 1975

She bought a wonderful dress for the premiere, black velvet, off the shoulder, ankle length. But no one noticed her.

It's been three years since she wrote *Diary*. Or is it five? Surely... it was longer than that? Yes! It was three years since Scotty. That heartbreak.

Her photograph wasn't taken. She sat through the premiere, stunned. With a kind of horror. Almost the first scene showed a sick-looking young woman waking up and drawing on a cigarette. She had the expression of a bag-lady, while her husband clattered about in expensive shoes and clothes, talking in a cheery, over-animated voice. Two resentful children (in her novel they were beautiful, lively little girls) mooched in and out of the plot. The lover, while attractive, hadn't an ounce of the toughness Emma had intended him to have – he seemed fey, almost effete. And there was barely any reference to Manhattan – when it was the city's punishing effects Emma had described. Had based the novel on.

With a fixed smile, she left the premiere, not joining the after-show party. Jonathan took her to an elegant, dark bar, where they had drinks and an Italian meal. Tears trickled down her face from time to time.

Never had she felt so disappointed, so betrayed.

The reviews were dismal.

Misery always made her think of heights. She'd always been attracted to heights. Cliff edges, high window ledges, bridges over rivers. At the same time, she was scared of them, but somehow there was an adrenalin rush when perching at the top of a cliff, knowing that one wrong move, one strong gust of wind, might just...

She remembered how, when she was an art student, she joined a tanker full of international students all going to Europe. A Dutch ship, crowded, an echoing loudspeaker several times a day – calling them to lunch, to dinner, warning them about this and that. After each announcement, the students sarcastically imitated the tinny Dutch voice, ending every announcement with, "Dank U... Dank U."

A day before they landed, she heard hysterical screams and saw students running all over the ship. A boy had fallen – or jumped – overboard while posing for a "trick shot". He'd done it for a bet of fifty dollars, someone said. She heard the words, "Man overboard!", saw the grim-faced Dutch crew, manning a lifeboat, lowered into the ocean. As the rescue boat slowly trawled on the waves, the ship was silent. Many of the girls were crying; impossible to think a body could be rescued from the Atlantic.

Yet he was spotted – a tiny black dot, raising an arm like Breughel's *Icarus* drowning. The lifeboat drew nearer and the boy was hauled from the water. The boy, green, gave a wan grin; there were a few cheers.

She sold a story based on this trip. But to risk death for a bet? If that was true, thought Emma. Would she do that for a bet? Of course not. Or only a bet with herself.

She moved round the apartment, still in her gown, sleeping a few hours, getting up for a while, and taking more slivers of pills.

Manhattan, 1977

The bad reviews for her last novel, and the film, had finished her, she said.

Which was ridiculous, Jonathan thought – there was so much in her life to be happy about, so much she could do. He knew it would finish her even more if he ever mentioned Freddy, their son.

All the signs were the kid had an exceptional brain: his cousins told him the boy had been a straight "A" student and excelled in fencing and violin classes. His big love was acting – he always had the main part in school productions. His idol was James Dean. He'd already had some small parts in TV series.

It was 1977. Emma was fifty. Her health had been declining for the past few years. How old fifty sounded. Without make-up, unwashed, she stared at herself in the mirror. Of course, she could wash her hair, put a facemask on, do her make-up, add blusher and contour... and she had no need to worry about her figure. But it had been "A Rough Year". The worst year yet. She hadn't written a word; despite the intervening years, the terrible reviews for *The Shrink Who Needed Me* still hurt. The film of *Diary*, she preferred to forget – or try to. A ghastly memory. Jonathan, rising ever higher in his job – now in line to be New York's most powerful, most prestigious doctor, chairing so many committees, doing so much research.

'I can help you, Em, and will help you any way I can – but you've got to help yourself,' he said. 'These depressions have been going on for years now. Think of them as simply an illness – an illness which can be treated. An illness from which you can recover. But you must help yourself as well.'

She felt she was a burden to him. She knew how he loved the social side of being an eminent medical professor – the clothes; the way he was known as both brilliant and elegant and, unlike her, up before six every day. She stayed in the apartment most of the time now, rarely getting dressed. She preferred not to see Carla. Or rather – she didn't want Carla to see her. She was aware of her coming in the morning, heard the sounds of cleaning and the washing machine threshing, the fridge being emptied and filled again with food to tempt her – fruits, protein shakes, salad, sea foods.

When she emerged from her bed, Carla had left, leaving a gleaming kitchen, shining bathroom, piles of freshly ironed laundry, and fresh flowers in pretty jugs; Jonathan's room as pristine as a five-star hotel. Only Emma's room was a mess – she didn't want Carla to see it. Of course, she put her laundry out to be done, and tried to change the sheets, when she felt strong enough; and she regularly rounded up the glasses, cups and plates she'd used, and left them in the kitchen. Piles of books heaped up by her bed. Jonathan brought her glossy magazines and newspapers – they mounted up in a chaotic muddle.

She often showered and got up about five o clock in the evening, but not always. Instead of clothes, she put on a fresh gown and pajamas. She could use a manicure, a pedicure – but the effort involved in going to a beauty parlor would be huge. In the evening she often felt a little better, a little more optimistic. If Jonathan was there, they might have a glass of wine together – though he was regularly speaking at a dinner, chairing a seminar. As the sun fell, she often thought her depression was lifting – yet the next morning, when she woke, the same old panic and dread.

She tried looking at art books: surely the paintings she loved would make her feel better? Her favorite pictures were all those on the Icarus theme – the erotic possibilities; the sheer glamor of the falling, dying, exquisite body surrounded by beautiful women. Angels. Erotic angels. Some reminded her of Mikey...

Jonathan suggested she try "group therapy" – what a joke! – to see if she'd find something for a new story. Something to stimulate her writing. Get her out of bed. His own view of it was scathing.

'My belief is only hospital treatment can cure – these damned talking therapies are a lot of hot air. In any case, there is so much the individual can do to extend their life span – exercise, work, interests, the right food and drink, not thinking too much about themselves, not becoming addicted to anything.'

Really. Fascinating.

'I don't mean to sound smug, Em, but I'm working on vital research on figures of avoidable deaths in the city now. It's exciting stuff – people could extend their lives with ease by living more carefully. I know we've got away from the subject of your group therapy plan – which I happen to think is great. It could make you a great story.'

It was your plan, Jonathan.

She thought she'd try it, as a kind of research. Jonathan had said, though he wasn't keen on "talking cures", certain kinds of more off-beat therapy could work.

'You could write a story about it,' he suggested. Maybe she could. Looking on it as "material" and not "medicine" made it better.

She went along, keeping her writer's notebook updated after every session. Intending to. She wrote in it once. She went along once.

Depressed? Can't sleep? Broken heart? My six-week women-only Heartbreak Healer course will soothe you. Uplifting and inspiring. I'd been dumped by an ex-rock star. I needed the Heartbreak Healer.

'Brilliant, Em!' said Jonathan when he read it. 'I think you could try that one on Harpers or Vogue, couldn't you? Promising! Are you going to finish it? Who did you base the rock star on who broke your heart?'

'No one. And I don't think I'll finish it,' she said.

'Try and finish things, Em. You'll feel so much better.'

She stuck her tongue out at his retreating back. She was beginning to really dislike him – yet every now and then the old awe returned.

*

She tells Jonathan she'll never write another novel.

Between the terrible reviews for her last novel and the crushing reviews for the movie, she finds no comfort. Eve tries to bolster her.

'You're now a name, Emma. Your first novel has been translated into nineteen languages and the film has been shown in five European countries. You've had many letters from readers who loved the books, and the movie – invitations to do talks, readings, workshops. Did you imagine this ten, twenty years ago? The thing is, build on it – don't let temporary blows defeat you, Emma.'

But she refuses all interview offers, doesn't care to do any talks, wouldn't run a workshop for a million dollars. She's starting to feel ill – really ill – rest, sleep is her only comfort. She thinks about Scotty – or is it Mikey? – a lot. Pretends he's in her arms. Dreams about him. In her dreams he's always living with them, smiling, playing.

Jonathan lay back on the couch, but didn't relax. On his desk, his therapist had a little gold-colored Buddha, which seemed out of place. The surgery – clinic – whatever he called it – was elegantly "done". The tiny Buddha looked like something cheap you lowered a little crane onto in an amusement arcade, and after twenty or thirty goes you picked something up.

If this doesn't work, I'll have to... have to have her... he thought, but said, 'I can't take much more. Emma's not just depressed – she's ill. But – she doesn't want any medical help. She stays in bed most of the time now – her room's a mess – eats very little, but has short periods now and then, or she did, where she gets up and will perhaps have a glass of wine and say a few words. That's mostly in the evening.'

Even as he spoke, Jonathan knew his words sounded as though Emma was unhinged.

'It's not that she's crazy,' he said. 'She gets so terribly depressed. Despite her novels, despite the film. Oh, I know all the reviews weren't dazzling. But so what? Many writers never even get reviews. Most writers would give a lot to be where she is.'

'Let's talk about you rather than Emma, for now. What's the effect on you?'

'I'm worried, damn it! I can't seem to do a thing. She won't take my advice, she never goes out. I have to attend all the dinners and events on my own – of course that's a minor part of it – we rarely have meals together, conversations. A vacation would be Herculean for her. Although Carla does the housework, I'm turning into almost... a carer. Emma is an intelligent and beautiful woman – she has more novels to write, I'm sure – but I never see her in anything but pajamas, looking terrible. She barely eats. She takes a lot of pills, painkillers, tranquilizers, sleeping pills – but not to any regime. She uses them as and when. She won't admit how much or what she takes. I don't think the doses are high, but they're mixed up.'

'Jonathan, I'm a psychoanalyst – shouldn't you be talking to a psychiatrist? Someone at the hospital, even a colleague? Someone who deals in depressive illnesses? Of course, I'm willing to see you – yet I feel this is a medical problem. Emma doesn't see her own therapist now, does she?'

'She hasn't left the apartment for weeks. Sometimes she stays in her room for days.'

'Forgive me – does she care about her looks, hygiene? I'm sorry – but these are markers to the degree of gravity of the illness.'

'Her looks, no – and she used to care a lot, she was always immaculate. But she doesn't often wash her hair or ever put make-up on. She manages a shower about every other day, not always. She may go four days staying in bed.'

'Then this is a medical problem, Jonathan. You've told me before about her depressions, but these were temporary? Depressions she managed to get over?'

'Something always happened to lift her out of them – a new book deal, the film, being offered some journalism. She's always uplifted by work. But that hasn't happened lately.'

'Is her agent in contact with her?'

'Eve has rung, but I've always made some excuse – said Emma has a migraine, or she's away, or we have family over. I think it would be a bad idea for her work contacts to know how depressed she is. Or even her friends.'

'So no one else knows how ill she is?'

'No one. I think it would be a mistake.'

'Why?'

'Well, I... what would it look like? As a writer she needs to keep a reliable profile. She wouldn't thank me for telling people – she'd be horrified. She hates being depressed.'

'It sounds as though the fact she's depressed is making her even more depressed.'

'Something like that. Thing is – what do we do?'

'I can't answer that. My only advice is to seek medical help for Emma, maybe from a trusted colleague. There are some good treatments now... but she'd need to go into a unit. And that would give you some respite, as well.'

'I can't think how I can put it to her. I feel so disloyal, like I should be able to solve her depressions myself – almost as if it's my fault.'

'I've had clients in similar positions. They all feel like that – as if they're letting their wives down by trying to help them. It's not the case.'

Jonathan noticed a vase of peonies and roses in the room – two of Emma's favorite flowers. And a painting by Rothko, he thought – Emma would know, of course. One wall was lined with bookshelves. He noticed Emma's books there.

'You've read Emma's work?'

'Indeed. Emma is a fine writer, a fine person. We met at a literary gathering. She mentions therapy in her fiction, taking a comic view – good. I was impressed. I'm sad she is so troubled. Practical measures are needed.'

'Yes. I know. It's just I'm so reluctant. The effect it would have on her – Christ.'

'But what effect will it have on her if she remains in this state, gets worse? I think you should talk to a colleague who deals in depressive illness – see what they say. Maybe you can present it to her as the medical equivalent of a spa break, something to relax and restore her energies, lift her depression. Maybe make the point that it's illness, not madness. For your own sake as well, you need to do this.' He tapped his pen against a folder. 'Could you do that, Jonathan? Taking action is so much better than taking no action.'

'And if she won't go into a hospital?'

'Cross that bridge when you come to it.'

Jonathan knew his hour was up. And that his therapist hadn't a clue as to the solution.

In the dream, she's walking along the cliff edge and carrying a little puppet. They're both wearing school uniform, and the puppet is talking to her.

'Don't let me go, Emma. Don't drop me,' it says in a voice a bit like her own, but squeakier.

'Of course I won't!' She clutches the puppet closer, even though she doesn't really like it.

It's a sunny day in her dream and she can clearly see the blue sky, the foaming waves. There's no hedge on the cliff – it's a sheer drop. There are waterfalls running down to the ocean, butterflies, and birds – like a Disney film.

'I said don't drop me, Emma!' the puppet orders. 'Your hand's getting loose. Hold me tighter!'

She is loosening her grip, at which the puppet screams.

'Stop it, Emma! You're joking, aren't you? You are joking?'

'I'm not... joking,' she gasps and sends the screaming puppet over the cliff edge.

Because it's only a puppet, no one cares. School friends stroll up to her.

'What happened?' says one.

'Nothing,' she says, but she can see the puppet far below, floating, in the blue school summer dress with red piping. And she thinks she can hear the puppet too.

I'll get you, Emma! I'm coming to get you!

The vicious cry, followed by terrible laughter.

In the dream, she feels herself fainting with fear, yet at the same time managing to grasp a thought.

It's only a dream... I can wake up.

She does wake up, shaking, sweating. She sips water. Takes a pill. She sinks back gratefully. Looks at her watch – 3 a.m. – maybe seven whole hours before she has to try to get up. Seven hours of peaceful darkness. Night.

'I'm not feeling well, Jonathan – I'll stay in bed today,' she says when he comes in. She's been saying that a lot lately. All the time? She doesn't remember.

'Wouldn't some air help, Emma? I've brought you some coffee. It's the start of that conference today – the one I'm chairing. It's way across town – I may be a little late... Carla's in today – she'll fix you some lunch.'

'I don't want any.'

'Please try, you're starting to look awfully thin.'

'You can never be too thin.'

'You can, actually.'

*

It's funny how he doesn't sound so sympathetic any more. She reaches for her old photograph of Mikey for comfort. It's nearly thirty years old now, that photo... she remembers how happy she was. He stayed with her – wasn't that it? And then died in a motorbike accident, only months later – Cathy told her.

There was a guitar-shaped wreath at his funeral.

She did manage a letter to her best friend, Ruth. A sort-of jaunty letter. The way they used to talk to each other:

> *It's been a very rough couple of months. A rough year. Couple of years.*
>
> *The critical reviews of* Shrink– *with that insane review in the British* Sunday Times – *did not help. I'm terribly happy you liked it. So many people did, do, and I am glad I wrote it. Although you won't catch me writing about the American family scene again soon. I felt I said something that hasn't been said – and have a raft of letters from women to prove it. The sad thing about the Women's Lib movement is that it has unleashed a backlash, of sorts – and the subject of The Unhappy Middle-Class Woman is almost taboo... We're on the verge of the 80s now, aren't we? Something's lost in writing. I'm not sure anything's gained.*

The phone rings.

Mia. One of her good friends.

'Emma, it *is* you! I've been ringing for days, for ever, but can never get you. I did get Jonathan, but he said you'd flown to L.A. Not like you – you hate flying. How are you?'

Her bright voice kicks in. Why did Jonathan lie? She'd no more get on a plane these days than enter a lion's cage. Why did he tell Mia that?

She knew, of course. He was ashamed of her depression. He didn't want anyone to know. Just how bad it was. How ill she was. Ashamed of her.

'I'm fine! I went to L.A. to give a little talk. I have been a bit unwell, but things are much better now. The bad reviews and... things.'

'You're feeling better?'

'I am, yes.'

'Going out?'

'Sure. I've been to a couple of movies and talks at MoMA. And been for a few dinners with Jonathan. He's been so good about this... thing.'

'Oh, everyone gets depressed from time to time. All writers do. It comes with the territory. The great thing is, it goes.'

'Yes – I'm working on a new story now.'

'Terrific! I'm so thrilled to hear that.'

'Yes – I'm managing five hundred words a day, at least.'

They chatted for a while longer. Emma replaced the phone, exhausted. The effort of being bright, cheery. She didn't feel any better. She got up, pulled on her robe, went to the kitchen.

'Mrs. Bowden!' said Carla. 'Could you manage some lunch today? I bought cream of watercress soup, the best there is. I've made baked chicken with fresh peaches and roast potatoes with rosemary – then a homemade coconut ice. Can I tempt you?'

She knew Jonathan would eat it today or tomorrow, or Carla could freeze it.

'All I really want is coffee and a biscuit. You have some lunch, Carla, and leave the rest in the ice box.'

'Dr. Bowden did ask me to try and interest you in having something to eat.'

'Too bad.'

She went back to bed.

Jonathan had seen a colleague, as advised by his shrink. He'd outlined Emma's state. The colleague told Jonathan he'd be "shooting from the hip".

'Jonathan, I'm not going to mince words. She needs hospital help – as soon as you can get her in. I'm a little surprised you've let this go on so long – but get her in soon, for Christ's sake.'

Sitting at Emma's bedside, Jonathan took a large gulp of his drink – then made the suggestion.

'Would you consider some hospital help? They have excellent treatments now – it's not the bad old days. Don't look like that please, Emma, and anyway, you don't need *that* – but it's a chance to try out some new drugs and procedures, really rest, eat a good diet and be free from any chores or worry. And of course, I'd come to see you every day. And I'm only talking a week or so. A luxury, private place, kind of, that's used to dealing with your illness. The statistics show many more people suffer from depression. But, Emma, you have to co-operate, and nobody need know. Ever. I'll keep it hushed up. I'll say you are at a health spa – which you could also enjoy after you've had the hospital treatment.'

'Please, Jonathan, stop it – I couldn't bear it,' she cried. 'I'll see a new shrink tomorrow – or the day after – and see if they have new treatments. There's something called hypnotherapy. It's a way of thinking that makes you feel more optimistic.'

Slowly, he drained his glass.

'Emma, I don't think you realize quite how ill you are,' he said gently. 'I can tell from your looks – and the state of your room – and your general demeanor how rarely you get up. How you never go out. And you take pills randomly – that's self-medication. You need to follow a regime, not just throw them down when you feel depressed. Don't you want to feel better, be your old self?'

What old self? Her old self was successful, achieving – and Jonathan loved her then. Now she was a millstone. He'd rather be with another doctor, some bright woman specialist who also loves after-dinner speaking and wears designer clothes. Who's written important research. Who's busy and happy. Who doesn't spend weeks in bed. She'd guessed.

She doesn't blame him, not really.

'I don't deserve to be my old self. Don't deserve it,' she whispered.

'For God's sake, Emma! What the hell are you saying?'

'I'm so... Jonathan, I don't want to go into hospital.

Please let me try something else... anything... I will get up early tomorrow, clean my room, go out.'

But the next morning she felt as bad – worse – and stayed in bed, until hunger drove her to the kitchen when Carla had left. She drank a chocolate shake, ate two chocolate biscuits, a banana. Then what? She started to cry, sobbing hysterically. She rang Jonathan at work, crying – something she'd never done before.

'I feel so ill... nothing's working. It's as though I don't exist.' She screamed with fright. 'Help me!'

He was calm.

'Emma, I'm coming home now. Try having a bath then go to bed, or rest on the sofa. I will be home soon, I promise.'

She had the bath, went back to bed, her refuge, her place.

When Jonathan came in, she was sleeping – she woke.

'Emma, have you taken anything?' he said.

'Yes... no... I... I can't remember. I think so, yes, a tiny piece of a sleeping pill. I think.'

'We can't go on like this. I've booked you into Payne Whitney for the day after tomorrow. For a week to start with. I'm certain you'll get well again. Carla will pack for you; all you have to do is get up and get dressed, something casual. Pack books – you'll have plenty of time to read and rest. I've already let them know the foods and drinks and flowers you like. They're looking forward to meeting you. I promise it's not as bad as you think. Please, Emma. Please.'

She saw it was inevitable. She did deserve it. Hadn't her parents always said she was a bad girl, not as good as other children, not deserving gifts, treats? She recalled an exchange trip in Europe that every single girl in her class was allowed to go on – but not her.

'Your behavior isn't good enough. Going out with boys all the time. You don't deserve it.'

Then when every girl in the class had a "junior" bra, her mother refused to buy her one. When she did give Emma one, it was something from a thrift store, gray and faded. The other girls had new matching sets in bright colors and patterns. So pretty.

And then when she had her first real boyfriend, her mother was unpleasant and suspicious.

'What are you doing until ten o'clock at night? You be careful, Emma. I don't doubt you're doing something wrong. And we don't want to be woken up by you coming in late and the door banging every night.'

When her first story was published, she'd had one letter from her mother:

> *I saw your short story in* The Post, *but of course no one really reads that. It's not as though it was* McCall's *or* Harpers *– can't you get something in those? Your father and I didn't really follow it – it seemed slow – though I guess it's supposed to be clever. Well done, anyway.*

No, she deserved nothing. She'd go to the psychiatric hospital.

*

It was June. Sunny, bright. She lay in bed, some tiny comfort from the soft pillows, the cool sheets, the scent of some linen fragrance Carla used when ironing. Waking was always a surprise – 'Me? Here?' – and after a few seconds, terror.

She hadn't been able to face clearing up her room – books, magazines and clothes scattered around, a sprawl of cosmetics on the dressing table, various used glasses and cups. Many bits of pills – so many she no longer knew what each segment was supposed to do.

She took three or four slivers, gulping them down with three day old water. She lay back. Oh, to sleep. Just to sleep. If only it was winter, not June, when the dark days made it more – usual – to sleep. Didn't people sleep through the winter in the Middle Ages? She'd read that, maybe even studied it some time. They began to get up when the spring came. To go about their business...

She lost the thread of her thoughts. And remembered with a shock of horror – tomorrow she was booked to go into the psychiatric hospital. It was all arranged. Jonathan would go with her in a taxi at 11 a.m. She needn't even pack – someone would do it for her. All she needed was to pick out personal things and a few books.

This can't be happening.

She picked up a hand mirror she kept by her bed and stared at her reflection. The hollowed-out cheeks, the dents under the eyes, the limp hair, the crow's feet. All the vitality and energy had drained from her. Her skin was pale, dry.

A lipstick had rolled onto the floor – she could reach it. She painted on a red mouth with a shaking hand. She thought she looked like a clown. How could she go to a place where people would see her? She didn't even have the energy to wash her hair or clean her teeth.

'How did it come to this?' she cried out loud. The pill she'd taken seemed to be making her feel worse, heavier, and without hope. She remembered the Vassar girls who'd died in a joint suicide, their arms lovingly entwined, their black silk nightdresses fresh, their faces made up. How right they were, to do it when they were young and fit. For them it was an adventure, an experiment in living – dying. They never went through pain, defeat, despair, menopause, rejection... they left when everything was bright. But poor Mikey – she looked at his picture again. She left it where Jonathan would find it. Take care of it.

She couldn't bear to ring Jonathan. He'd arranged everything for tomorrow. She couldn't tell him she wouldn't be going to that place. She imagined it – nurses with fake, cheerful faces, hair bunned up, crisp white uniforms, a private room that Jonathan would arrange to have filled with flowers, as though she was already dead. Having to talk to earnest therapists for real – she never thought of her shrink appointments as more than a kind of luxury; everyone in Manhattan had a shrink – having to explain her thoughts, submit to treatments. Maybe – even electric treatment?

She tried to push this thought away. This horror. Pains – stomach cramps – started up. Like period pain, yet they couldn't be that now.

Perhaps – all the different bits of pills she'd swallowed?

Air. She needed air.

She swallowed one paracetamol to try to ease the pain – maybe three, four. She moved to the balcony rail.

Emma! We're here!

'I'm coming,' she whispers.

EPILOGUE

Emma was buried in a secret grave in New York. The funeral details were never announced. Jonathan did not reply to any letters of condolence from her friends, or speak to them ever again. He went on to harness international acclaim as a medical professor – and of course became New York's most eminent doctor. He gave many television and press interviews about his work, but refused to talk about Emma. Five years after Emma's death, he married a woman surgeon.

ACKNOWLEDGEMENTS

With much love and warmest thanks to all the friends who inspired, helped and encouraged me:

Andrés Bolado, Sarah Bayliss, Jean Burnett, Adrian Colston, Jenny Longhurst, Shirley Hewson, Crysse Morrison, Clare Reddaway, Graham Ryan, Judith Spelman, Jay Merrick, Michael Spurgeon, John Skuse, Derek Williams. Also in loving memory of my grandmother, Beatrice Maggs, and my father, Jim Cambridge. And for Clare B.

Grateful thanks to the Louise Walters Books team who did a wonderful job with their meticulous and creative work: Jennie Rawlings, Leigh Forbes and Alison Jack… thank you all so much. And of course to Louise, for her endless patience, support and most of all, belief in me.

The book is inspired by the life and work of the late Manhattan author Sue Kaufman, whose writing I've loved for decades. Kaufman fans might recognise some aspects of that unique Kaufman territory… but it's a work of imagination.

ALSO FROM LOUISE WALTERS BOOKS

Louise Walters Books is the home of intelligent, provocative, beautifully written works of fiction. We are proud of our impressive list of authors and titles. We publish in most genres, but all our books have one aspect in common: the high quality of the writing.

Further information about all LWB books and authors can be found on our website:

louisewaltersbooks.co.uk

FALLIBLE JUSTICE
Laura Laakso

"I am running through the wilderness and the wilderness runs through me."

IN OLD LONDON, WHERE paranormal races co-exist with ordinary humans, criminal verdicts delivered by the all-seeing Heralds of Justice are infallible. After a man is declared guilty of murder and sentenced to death, his daughter turns to private investigator Yannia Wilde to do the impossible and prove the Heralds wrong.

Yannia has escaped a restrictive life in the Wild Folk conclave where she was raised, but her origins mark her as an outsider in the city. Those origins lend her the sensory abilities of all of nature. Yet Yannia is lonely and struggling to adapt to life in the city. The case could be the break she needs. She enlists the help of her only friend, a Bird Shaman named Karrion, and together they accept the challenge of proving a guilty man innocent.

So begins a breathless race against time and against all conceivable odds. Can Yannia and Karrion save a man who has been judged infallibly guilty?

*

This is fantasy at its literary, thrilling best, and is the first title in Laura Laakso's paranormal crime series Wilde Investigations. There is a wonderfully human element to Laura's writing, and her work is fantasy for readers who don't like fantasy (or think they don't!) and it's perfect, of course, for those who do.

Available in paperback, ebook, and audio.

The Last Words of Madeleine Anderson

Helen Kitson

"Writing is like a love affair, or should be. You get to know your story, it intrigues you, if you're lucky it enthrals you, and ultimately it ends, leaving you wretched and abandoned."

ONCE UPON A TIME Gabrielle Price wrote and published an extraordinary novel.

But twenty years on her literary star has dimmed, her "work of genius" is all but forgotten, and no further novels have materialized. She now lives an unremarkable life: middle-aged, living alone in the sleepy village she grew up in, and working as a housekeeper for the local vicar. Her lonely existence is dominated by memories of her best friend Madeleine, who died young, in tragic and mysterious circumstances.

Gabrielle's quiet world is turned upside down when she meets and befriends Simon – young, attractive, a would-be writer, and enthusiastic fan of the astonishing novel that Gabrielle published all those years ago. Charmed and flattered, she recklessly invites him into her home and her heart. But Simon is mysterious and manipulative, and it's not long before he forces Gabrielle to confront the demons in her past. Gabrielle's obsession begins to destroy her carefully cultivated life, and she comes to feel increasingly threatened by Simon's presence. Who is he? Why did he seek her out? And what does he really want?

*

The debut novel from acclaimed poet Helen Kitson is a joy to read: mysterious, reflective, and darkly humorous. Diana Cambridge describes it as "Barbara Pym noir".

Available in paperback, ebook, and audio.

ECHO MURDER

Laura Laakso

"I'm part of every bird I meet, and they are all within me."

YANNIA WILDE RETURNS to the Wild Folk conclave where she grew up, and to the deathbed of her father, the conclave's Elderman. She is soon drawn back into the Wild Folk way of life and into a turbulent relationship with Dearon, to whom she is betrothed.

Back in London, unassuming office worker Tim Wedgebury is surprised when police appear on his doorstep with a story about how he was stabbed in the West End. His body disappeared before the paramedics' eyes. Given that Tim is alive and well, the police chalk the first death up to a Mage prank. But when Tim "dies" a second time, Detective Inspector Jamie Manning calls Yannia and, torn between returning to the life she has built in Old London and remaining loyal to the conclave and to Dearon, she strikes a compromise with the Elderman that allows her to return temporarily to the city.

There she sets about solving the mystery of Tim's many deaths with the help of her apprentice, Karrion. They come to realise that with every death, more of the echo becomes reality, and Yannia and Karrion find themselves in increasing danger as they try to save Tim. Who is the echo murderer? What sinister game are they playing? And what do they truly want?

*